A Guide to Being Born

A Guide to Being Born

STORIES

Ramona Ausubel

RIVERHEAD BOOKS

a member of Penguin Group (USA) Inc.

New York

2013

RIVERHEAD BOOKS
Published by the Penguin Group
Penguin Group (USA) Inc., 375 Hudson Street,
New York, New York 10014, USA

USA · Canada · UK · Ireland · Australia
New Zealand · India · South Africa · China

Penguin Books Ltd, Registered Offices:
80 Strand, London WC2R 0RL, England
For more information about the Penguin Group visit penguin.com

The following stories have been previously published in slightly different form:
"Atria" (*The New Yorker*), "Poppyseed" (*FiveChapters*), "Safe Passage" (*One Story* and
Best American Fantasy 2009), "Saver" (*pax americana*), "Snow Remote" (*Slice*
magazine), "The Ages" (*Orange Coast Review*), "Tributaries" (*Electric Literature*),
"Welcome to Your Life and Congratulations" (*Green Mountains Review*)

Library of Congress Cataloging-in-Publication Data

Ausubel, Ramona.
[Short stories. Selections]
A guide to being born / Ramona Ausubel.
p.   cm
ISBN 978-1-59448-795-8
I. Title.
PS3601.U868G85   2013   2013002037
813'.6—dc23

Printed in the United States of America
1   3   5   7   9   10   8   6   4   2

BOOK DESIGN BY AMANDA DEWEY

For Teo and Clay, my loves

Contents

BIRTH

Safe Passage

THE GRANDMOTHERS—dozens of them—find themselves at sea. They do not know how they got there. It seems to be afternoon, the glare from the sun keeps them squinting. They wander carefully, canes and orthotics, across the slippery metal deck of the ship, not built for human passage but for cargo. Huge shipping crates are stacked at bow and stern. The grandmothers do not know what it means. *Are we dead?* they ask one another. *Are we dying?* Every part of the ship is metal, great sheets and hand-sized rivets. Cranes and transverses and bulkheads and longitudinals—all metal. All painted white and now splayed with the gray stars of gull droppings.

Among the many hunched backs and stockinged legs, there is a woman named Alice, who finds the nicest bench and sits down on it. The bench looks out at the horizon, that line drawn by the eye to make an ending where there is not one. Alice is a lover of views, of great expanses, and she is happy now as she has always been, to look out. She thinks of her children on faraway spits of land. They have their studios and paints, their meditation cushions, their cars in need of oil changes and their grocery lists. She thinks about her one new great-granddaughter whom she has never met but who she hopes is wrapped in the gray blanket she knit.

Around Alice there are varying levels of commotion and flurry. *Does anyone have a compass? Do you know how to drive a ship? Where is my nurse? I'm from the DC area!*

There are some grandmothers who try to escape immediately. They get in a rescue craft tied to the side of the ship and sit holding their pocketbooks, waiting patiently to be lowered down to the tattered blue. Their faces become wet with wind-water, but they are not lowered. Their hairdos begin to wilt, but still, they do not get lowered.

There is the group of ladies whose eye makeup travels in dark tracks down cheeks; the group of proactive grandmothers who have taken scraps of paper and pens from their pocketbooks and are brainstorming a list of suggestions, diagramming these suggestions in order of popularity and feasibility. In front of Alice is the group of rememberers, recounting as if centuries had passed, their lives. *It used to be so easy*, they remember at high volume due to a common loss of hearing. *There were lovely smooth roads, and it was possible to get in the car and drive to different places where the pancakes were especially good, where the coffee was flown in from Italy.*

But even in this situation, extraordinary and new, even with the churning ocean surrounding them completely, many of the grandmothers make small talk. They compliment each other's earrings. *Are those pearls freshwater? The color reminds me of the curtains my mother bought on a trip to Bangkok, where she met the princess, if you can believe that.*

Alice is joined by someone whose name she does not even listen to. The woman says, "You are from Chicago, you say. How *is* Chicago this time of year?"

"Well, it's very cold on one day and then it's very warm the next day."

"And your children, what do they do?"

"I have two painters, a woodworker and a writer."

"How *interesting*," the woman says. "Mine are all lawyers. I have six."

"My father was a lawyer." Alice smiles. "It was a terrible way to grow up. I'm glad none of mine went that way." The woman's facial muscles seem to harden but are subverted by the skin hanging soft, always, no matter how tight her smile or her frown.

"It's possible I'm dead," Alice says, looking at the differing blues of sky and water.

"I'm sorry." Though the woman is looking at Alice, she seems to be most sorry for herself.

Alice nods. "Yes, I guess I might have died. Or be dying." She remembers a hospital room and behind the bed a wall of machines, each emitting a very distinct beep that would draw a different nurse with a different tool. One brought Linda with a suction pump that gathered, painfully, the mucus from Alice's lungs. One brought Kera with a new bag of liquid food to be attached to the feeding tube. The room was always half dark, permanent evening. At all times at least one of her relatives was in the room.

Uneasily, the woman comforts, "I'm sorry to hear that."

Alice nods again and stretches her legs out, covered in the skin of stockings, and wiggles her feet at the ends.

"Am I dead too, then?"

"I don't know. Did you die?" Alice asks.

"I don't remember dying."

"Well, maybe you didn't."

UNDER THE SETTING SUN, the ship is stained red. The deck looks like a high school cafeteria with small clusters of ladies huddled close together, constellated out over the surface. They remember to worry about things they had forgotten to worry about at first. The slippery surface is of great concern to many who fear the breaking of hips. They fret over husbands, who have been left at home with nothing in the refrigerator. Cats are likely pawing the heavy legs of couches. The couches will never survive the absence of the grandmothers. This will be the end of the couches. They talk about this. They huddle against the wind.

Some grandmothers who are quiet in the huddles do not have these things to go back to. Some have not turned off their televisions in years, not in the morning or at night. They have freezers full of food ready-packed for quick eating, and the dents in the cushions where they sit all day, their faces dimming and brightening in the light, are severe. The dents do not re-puff, because they do not have a chance to do so. They are always under-butt. These grandmothers nervously check their watches still set to home-time, knowing that right now, right at this moment when the sun is falling, Pat Sajak is about to welcome them, with the help of his generous audience, to Wheel!

Of! Fortune! Even though they will miss this television evening, those grandmothers, the ones with no one, are not so sorry to be here at sea with so many warm bodies.

While they trade stories of survival, the proactive grandmothers who have no time for idle worrying are on a mission to find out what is inside the crates on deck. A set of bolt cutters has been discovered in the engine room. The engines were discovered there as well but were much too complicated to operate, so the ship continues to float, unrumbling.

These women have been in strange situations before. "In Bermuda," someone says, fingering the gold buttons on her cardigan, "right in the middle of our perfect vacation, a hurricane hit and we had to take the little girl who sold shell jewelry into our hotel room for two straight days. Poor thing had never had a Pepsi cola before," she recalls. "Can you imagine?" the fellow proactive grandmothers marvel.

Alice, meanwhile, walks the edge of the boat, passing a lady whose hands are busy clenching. "Hullo," she says, nodding to the woman, the rail holder. The look she gets is a short, hopeful one, one that wants to see a man, any man, but a man in uniform especially. Any man in uniform with some kind of list. When she looks up to see another sagging female, she deflates.

Alice has been on a lot of boats. While she runs her hand along the railing, she remembers the first time and the last— love early, love late. When she was seventeen years old, after an expensive wedding at her parents' country house with none of her friends in attendance, she spent the first week as a wife on a sloop off the coast of Rhode Island. The first night, after navigating out of a very tricky harbor in a storm, her victorious husband came into the cabin where Alice was curled up. The small boat tossed in the heavy wind.

"I would rather we went back," she managed. "We're very far away from anything."

"The tide is against us. The dangerous thing would be to go back," he began, drying his glasses on a towel.

She insisted—she told him she couldn't stand it out there. "Please," she said.

He put the sail up and started the journey back. Alice, inside, did not see the work he did to take her in. She did not see the boat list and scoop water onto his bare feet.

With the sound of the dock squeaking against the hull, they lay side by side, he reading by candlelight, she pretending to sleep, with only two ropes holding them steady.

In the morning she tried to be a wife. She got an egg from the small icebox and cracked it into the pan, but the yolk broke and bled. The yellow heart ran rivers over the white. She turned the heat off and left it there, dying. Alice jumped in the water in her nightgown and swam to the small dinghy attached to the hull of their boat, where she bobbed, her clothes sucked to her body.

"What are you doing?" her husband yelled when he found her. She did not answer. He reeled her craft in until it knocked against his. "Did you swim out?" he asked, putting his hands on her wet head. "You could have put on a bathing suit."

"I am not a good wife."

"You can learn." They sat in silence, the sound of water dripping off her and landing in the belly of the vessel. "You stay here in your own little ship. You don't have to be anybody's wife here. I'll go make myself something to eat." He patted her and returned to his own boat, letting her rope go until she drifted back out to the maximum ten feet. The sea was a flat sheet going on until it couldn't anymore, until the sky pinned it down.

This was the beginning of a marriage that would continue into her fifties, when he left for good to start another family. She is sorry that she was not the one who pressed herself up against him to keep him warm when he was dying. Instead they corresponded by mail, and twice she sat on the porch swing outside his house with him and they talked about their children and their grandchildren, those lives they had made together, while his wife kept herself busy in the house.

Her second marriage was also more than thirty years long. He had said, "Please, there is no reason not to marry me. I am smart and kind and I will do the dishes." This wedding, just like the first, took place at her parents' house, only this time she was driven off in a golf cart instead of put on a sailboat.

They were retired for almost the entire duration, and for years before he died, they traveled often by freighter, where they were the only two paying passengers, sitting together on deck and doing the Jumble while the crew called commands to one another. Her husband couldn't see well as he got old, so she'd narrate the journey for him. "On the left there is an old fishing shack. It has fallen down on one side and the porch now hangs into the water. There are vines pulling it under. Two big birds are standing on the roof."

"Are they egrets?" he wanted to know.

"No, they are great blue herons."

"Oh, I was picturing egrets."

"Well, they aren't. But they *are* very nice-looking."

"I'm sure they are. I was just picturing egrets."

"Well, it doesn't matter now because that shack has passed. Now we are coming to a town. There are three little girls standing in the mud in their bathing suits, waving. Do you hear them calling to us?"

"Sort of." They both listened hard, the young voices making their way over the surface of the water.

"Do they have bicycles?" he asked.

"Why would they have bicycles?"

"Or fishing poles? How did they get there?"

"They just have hands. They are only trying to say hello."

"Well, hello then!" he called back. "Hello!" The two of them called together, their arms working back and forth like a pair of windshield wipers, trying to clear the view ahead.

WHEN ALICE'S CIRCUMNAVIGATION takes her around to the bow of the ship, she finds the proactive grandmothers surrounding the crates like flies. They are furious with curiosity about what is inside, what they are carrying with them on some unknown body of water. "Perhaps there are beautiful Chinese green beans or Italian leather coats," says one. "Maybe they are full of the most luxurious furs," tries another. "I think it will be jewels!" shrieks another, though this seems optimistic to everyone else.

What they find are none of those things. When the lock springs open on the first crate and the doors too, what they see inside are rows of white. Someone pulls, and to her feet fall five toilet seats. They are the padded kind, sighing under the weight of the sitter. There must be hundreds of them in there. This crate is quickly abandoned in disappointment, though Alice has put a toilet seat over her head and wears it, to everyone's enjoyment, like a necklace.

In the next crate they find child-size wooden baseball bats with the words "Sluggy Bat" written in wide cursive. This find interests no one, except one short lady who inches a bat out of the middle and swings it, remembering playing with her sisters in the street and pleased to find that it is a nice weight for her.

Crate number three is full—full!—of yellow roses. The grandmothers hug them in bundles to their chests, their arms pricked by the thorns. They distribute the flowers around— handing the wilting bouquets out to their fellow passengers until they all look like prom queens ready to dance their victory dance, the thorns freckling their arms with blood.

EVEN HERE, evening comes and then night. The grandmothers go inside to the galley, where they make their way through the first of many cases of canned peaches, sharing a single can opener found in a drawer. They discover that the toilet seats improve the comfort of the sitter on hard benches. They begin and end card games and word games. They quiz one another on presidential trivia. They begin to slump, exhausted.

Around them are the roses on the floor, the countertop, the cheap wood tables with names carved into them—Danny and Phoung, Rocko, the shape of a penis now covered by some blooms. Roses are worn behind ears and tucked into buttonholes. They smell as they are supposed to.

The grandmothers feel farther and farther away.

As they huddle, even under the wrap of polyester blankets taken from bunks, the work of their bodies is almost visible— the sinews of muscle responding again and again to the heart's insistence. Dozens of kerosene lanterns flicker, and the grand-mothers, whose eyes are falling shut but who do not want to go alone to their cabins, who fear that this might be *it* for them, begin to ask one another questions.

"Tell me the story of my life," someone asks. "Tell me what I was like when I was a baby." And they can do it. They get the details wrong—locations of birth, names of parents and siblings—but this does not matter to anyone. They chime in, an-swering together, bit by bit. "Your mother was so happy to meet you," someone says. "Your father brought the congratulatory tiger lilies right up to your new nose," another adds. They all close their eyes. "And you were such a good baby. You hardly ever cried." The many lips pull up into smiles. The grandmoth-ers remember even if they don't.

"And then when I was a child?" they ask together.

"Oh, when you were a child you had hair like an angel."

"You had a sweater your mother made with a picture of a rabbit knitted in."

"You were very good in arithmetic and you would have been good at the flute too." They cannot get enough of their lives.

"The fighting was mostly over money. It wasn't about you."

"Your mother did not mean to hit you in the eye with the serving platter. You just walked into it."

"Your granddad forgave you for getting lost in Puerto Val-larta that day."

"And your sister looked beautiful in her blue dress," a husky voice adds. The grandmothers, Alice among them, see the blue dress. Some see a silk navy A-line, some see a cotton sheath belted at the waist, some see an evening dress flicker out the door and into a waiting car. They are quiet in their rememberings.

"Who is there when I die?" someone asks, and they all nod to say yes, they wonder that too. Alice clears her throat and begins, confident.

"Your children are there," she tells them. "All of them. Three of your grandchildren too. They all have their hands on your body. You can feel them letting go of warmth. It doesn't stop at the skin or at the bone—nothing can stop it. They are singing 'Michael, Row the Boat Ashore.' Outside the window you can see a lake and a Ferris wheel on the edge. It is not raining outside but it looks like it might."

The grandmothers have wet eyes. They are all picturing themselves lying there with many pairs of hands covering them, more hands than possible, their bodies hidden. It is just the backs of hands, familiar and radiating and with very faint pulses. In their minds, the grandmothers dissolve under those palms. They go gaseous. It is no longer necessary to maintain any particular shapes.

Alice sits surrounded by the rattle of their collective breathing. These lungs are not noiseless machines anymore. In this close circle they are trading matter; molecules of one go straight into the tubes of another. Alice thinks of the ocean they are floating on, waves rolling out over the miles. And in those waves, fish in schools so large they turn the ocean silver.

"We are out at sea," she says. "We should not go to bed. We

should go fishing." The faces in the dim firelight are uncertain. "We are floating on top of a lot of creatures. Let's see what we catch," she tries to explain.

"We don't have any poles," a voice counters.

"We can make some," Alice responds. "We have no idea what might be down there!" Her voice is high and excited.

No one wants to be left alone, so they pull their blankets tighter, though it isn't cold. The women set to work unraveling strings from the salt-heavy ropes coiled like great snakes on deck. They isolate one string at a time and then tie them around the necks of some of the baseball bats. The grandmothers disperse along the railing and drop their very long lines. The lines have no hooks and no bait. Those lines on the port side, where the wind is coming from, are pasted to the hull like clinging lizards. Those lines on starboard blow out so that, all together, the row of them looks like the rib cage of a whale.

The women themselves are nearly invisible but for some moonlit glowings of hair—fuzzy little white islands in the dark. The sound of the overhead ring of gulls is mostly wing noise and an occasional vocal cry.

In the underneath, in that syrupy dark, the creatures they are trying to catch do not notice the tips of the hopeful strings. Jellies jet themselves along, not going anywhere, just moving for the sake of moving. Any fishes who can glow, glow. Some have patterns of light on their spines. Fake eyes look like real eyes for the purpose of being left alone. Sharks separate the water like curtains, currents flowing off their bared teeth.

There is always the chance of a giant squid and the great

likelihood of regular squid. The octopus must not need, in the dark hours, to dispense their ink. The ink stays churning inside the cool gut of the creature, all eight arms reaching and twisting and gathering. Miniature fish congregate and suck at the bodies of bigger fish, eating the growing algae. Turtles swim the length of entire oceans in order to lay their eggs on the beach where they were born.

The ship sloshes and the grandmothers sway. They keep their lines steady, most balancing the tiny baseball bats on their laps. They hum. Their voices are crackly and uneven. Some go for television theme songs. Some fumble over old lullabies. They don't mind that their melodies do not match up—it is nice to hear the humming and to do the humming, just to make noise. To feel the throat vibrating and air in the nose.

Alice is humming a lullaby invented by her own grandmother about a small horse when she feels a tug at her line. The song dies in her chest. She is holding on with both her hands, each one bearing a wedding ring—husband number one on her right and husband number two on her left. Her knuckles are pale hills, hunkered down, ready for anything. "Fish!" she calls. "Fish!" The other grandmothers shriek and repeat, "Fish! Fish!" They come to her, some faster than others.

"Stand up!" one yells. "Stand up and let me help you hold that bat." Alice stands. The woman comes in from behind, threading her arms through Alice's. The handle of the bat is held now by four hands and it looks like baseball practice, like the coach will, in slow motion, move Alice's arms in a perfect swing.

Instead they walk backward, leaning away from the railing. The rope tries to resist. More grandmothers join in, taking the line and hauling the thing up. Arms tire easily. There are those who stand on the sidelines and cheer. It is a long time before the pullers come to the sea-wet part of the rope.

When the thing finally flops onto the deck, they are surprised to see that built into the fish's forehead is a small pole with a fleshy light at the end, a greenish bulb. "You must have come from very far down," Alice says to the fish, "to have your own lantern." The grandmothers circle up, everything dark except the round light, which illuminates a gnash of long, sharp teeth. The heavy scales reflect the moonlight in vague arches. The fish is not content on deck. It flops its tail, slapping.

"I know that fish. That's an angler," one grandmother says.

"This fish really exists?" asks another.

"We should name it," someone ventures. "I'd like to name it Marty, after my husband." This is met with silence.

"I'd like to name it Harriet, after my mother," someone else tries.

"And I'd like to name it Marcello." They add names: Bill, Mort, Jesus, Kayla, Albert, Martha, Susan, Jeanette, Anne, Ned, Hank, as if throwing pennies into a fountain. The fish flops as it takes on the names of loved ones.

"It's my fish," Alice says, "and I am going to name him Fishy. But he can have all those others as middle names." This does not meet opposition. They stand there over him and do not speak, but in all their heads are prayers. They throw them at the scaled creature, at his round body, at his ugly face. They hope for the good ones to get what they deserve. They hope for the lost ones to get home, for the prices to go down, for more days in the backyard for everyone. Fishy's light goes a little soft and his eyes are dark liquid balls with shivers of moon inside. Alice bends down and picks the fish up. "Hello, Fishy," she says. She kisses her fingertips and touches them to its head. "I think we better throw you back now." She hobbles to the edge of the boat, tired after the long pull, while the knot of old ladies watches. She hums as she goes, returning to the lullaby about the horse. When she reaches the railing, she turns back to the huddle and holds Fishy up for his goodbyes.

"Goodbye!" "Goodbye, Neil!" "Goodbye, Albert!" "Goodbye, Nixon!" "Goodbye, Bill!" they chant. And out he goes. He does not hit the hull but makes a very straight, very fast journey back to the water, where he will continue to navigate the darkness with his green bulb. On deck some of the grandmothers kneel over the pool of water where Fishy had been. They dip their fingers in it and put it on their foreheads. They taste it, their dry old tongues bitten by the salt.

IT IS A WARM NIGHT and though the rest of the grandmothers go inside to their claimed cabins, Alice lies down on deck. She covers herself with her blanket. "I think tomorrow is Wednesday," she says to herself. "The garbage goes out on Wednesday." She can hear the sound of the truck, green and screeching as it devours up the trash and smashes it down. "It's the day I teach poetry, in my apartment." The day that she will not attend is laid out before her, the newspaper that she will not read lands at her doorstep. The phone, the refrigerator, the cat. She holds her own hands.

In a hospital room, four grown children surround their mother. Nervous, one eats a bag of chips. Another opens a book of poems, searches for the exact right words. The nurses prepare swabs, towels. Grandchildren collect around the bedside. It is not dark in the room but it is not light either, and even the city outside whispers. There are sailboats slipping along the surface of the lake. They tack around red buoys. The sailors' voices cannot be heard this high, this far away—the whole world between them—still their boats are part of this big view. When a telephone in the corner rings, the only son chats with two of his mother's oldest friends before he says, "They're going to take the tubes out of her lungs. Any minute." One daughter rubs her mother's hands with lotion. "It's in and out, just like this," she says, breathing to show breathing. "Go as long as you want. It can be two minutes and it can be ten years."

When the son hangs up the phone, he asks his mother, "Do you have any idea how many people adore you?" And this woman, this mother and grandmother, smiles wide enough that her teeth, treasures in that cave, shine.

THE BOAT IS ROCKING, the sea stretching around her.

"Do you think this is it?" Alice asks, but there is no answer. "There are people I was hoping to see again!" she calls out to the dark. Her knees are tucked together, legs folded like wings. Below, so much water moves restlessly. Above, the air does the same.

The gulls still circle even though it is too dark to hunt. "Do you know," Alice yells to the birds above, "that I have not been swimming in ages? How do you not swim in such a great big ocean?" Soon she is tying great knots along the enormous rope, every foot and a half. The knots are the size of her head. It gets harder and harder the farther she gets from the end. Her palms are sore. Each knot she ties, she tries to remember a person she loves. She gets the name and the face in her mind. The Jewish boy she wasn't allowed to see; her cousin, whom she always got in trouble with as a girl; her brother, whom she loved better than others did; her mother, who ended it all when she thought things were starting to get unsightly. Her two husbands, whose necks she could still smell, who had left her, one and then the next, alone on the turning earth. She thinks to herself, *Now I can say that I love them all. I am an old woman and no one will try to dissuade me.* All the single fibers, twisted together into ten, the ten into a hundred, the hundred into a thousand.

She takes her dress off and makes the trip in her white slip. She can feel the wind moving through her loose cotton underwear, but it is the slip that really dances. It puffs up and looks, at moments, like a wedding gown, then pastes itself to her body, every shape underneath mimicked by the fabric. The separation of the legs is defined along with the cut of the waist. The rope swings gently, and the clinging lady with it.

"I don't know if I can make it!" Alice calls up to the gulls.

She is more than halfway down. Again, as her feet move to a new knot, she remembers a person she loves.

Her feet slide to the next knot and hands follow.

Alice reaches the water. When she touches down, the water stings. "It's cold," she relays to the dry air. But she wants to let go of the rope. She wants to be free of the climb, so she lets herself fall in, her entire weight let loose in the water. It catches her easily and she dunks her head under. She laughs the laugh of a cold, floating person. She waves her arms and lets the yips come out of her mouth. She peers below, trying to see, but the only things are her own feet haloed by green phosphorescence, kicking and kicking and kicking.

"Will both of my husbands be mine again?" she calls to the birds or the fish or the sky. "Can I love them again now?" She does not get her answer. Her slip rises up around her like a tutu. She looks now like a ballerina on a music box, legs bared under the high-flying skirt. The material is soft and brushes Alice's arms. She does not try to hold the slip down. Her breasts float up. All around her the green light of stirred water.

The boat groans and leans away, then begins to slip across the smooth sea. Alice does not feel herself moving and the ship leaves no wake, yet there is much morning-bright water between them. Her rope slaps at the hull, quieter as it goes, until all she hears is the echo of a sound no longer taking place, just her ear's memory of that song. The ocean is full and the sky is full—how plentiful the elements are! Alice floats on her back at the exact point of their meeting, held like a prayer between two hands pressed together.

She dives under and spins, making a lopsided flip, and

emerges with her hair stuck to her face. Drops fall from her chin in a glowing chain. They fall from her hair and from her ears and from the tip of her nose. They fall from eyelashes and from the lobes of her ears. The drops join back up with the whole ocean and disappear inside that enormous body. Alice throws her arms up in ta-da position, water flying off in a great celebration of sparks.

Poppyseed

LAURA AND I CELEBRATED my new job for the sake of having something to celebrate. I picked up a mushroom pizza and a six-pack of Diet Cokes, and Laura and I sat on a picnic blanket in the middle of our suburban front yard. Poppy sat there too, only she was in her stroller bed as always. The grass was craning out of the dirt and the birds were going for all our scraps. We lay on our backs like Poppy does, flat down, and looked at the graying blue of the sky. It came at us. Storming us with its color, with its light.

That afternoon, when I accepted the job as the head guide of the ghost tour on the retired ocean liner, the boss told me I could write my own content for the tour. Mr. Peterson said, "We love that you are creative. We think that's so cool!"

I shook his hand and then I sat in the car and let go of a few tears. I had to. It was the first time anyone was paying me to write something and it was the worst kind of writing. Shameful, jokey, forgettable.

"Thank you for taking this job," Laura said, without turn-ing to look at me. "I know you don't want it."

"I don't not want it. I want to do whatever I need to do."

"Do you want to ever try again?" she asked, looking at her middle.

"We can't afford it."

"My mother would keep helping with money."

"That's not what I mean."

When the sun dropped behind the trees, their shadows got long and greedy. We went inside and threw away the rest of our dinner, kissed our mute and immobile kin good-night. Our stunted eight-year-old. She didn't meet our eyes, but she did make some noises; she did hold our fingers in each of her fists, Laura's in her right and mine in her left.

We stood there in a chain like that until she let go and re-leased us.

Dear Poppy,

I had to tell your father about the pubic hairs. I tried to call him at work, but I didn't get him—I couldn't put the news on his voice mail. I waited until he was home and we had eaten our dinner and I asked him, "How was work, honey?"

He said, "I got there on time and I left on time. I found a guy to install something that will make the ladders shake all at once in the boiler room. It's very loud."

"That's good, right?"

"They say that's good. Noise and light—my job."

We ate ice cream and held hands over you on the couch.

I said, "She's really growing up." He squinted at me.

"Are you joking?" he asked. "She's the same as always. She might look like a second grader, but really, she is exactly, exactly the same as always."

"She's longer," I said. "But also . . ." I pulled your pants down where, beyond the pink elastic-squeezed line, a few terrible hairs were pressed flat to your skin. He covered you quickly and closed his eyes. He isn't mad at you, Poppy. You are the size and shape of a regular eight-year-old, with a baby's brain. How could it be that your body is getting ahead? As we sat there looking over you, covered now, Roger kept saying your age, eight, to himself. Eight, eight.

"Her body doesn't have a plan," Dr. Keller told us on the phone. "Next she's going to get a period, you know." He sounded as if he was scolding us for eating too much sugar. Your father was on the phone in the kitchen and I was on the other line, sitting on our bed. I could hear him breathing through the wires.

"It sounds to me like her body does have a plan. It's a bad plan, but it's a plan," I said. "I guess you must have a better one?"

"We could do a hysterectomy. This is actually a no-big-deal procedure. Hundreds are done every day. She has no use for a uterus."

I imagined your organs, each slick and pumping

shape tucked inside you, with a hole in the middle. I wondered if the rest would ooze over into the new space, if they would grow bigger or else rattle around.

"And there is the possibility that breasts would cause further discomfort."

"You seem to have this all figured out," Roger said. I heard him in the phone and also in the house. I heard the chair squeaking under him.

The doctor told us a story of you later, at a time when you have grown too big to lift and we have hired a large caretaker to help out, and this person happens to be a man and he brushes up against you one day and your nipples harden. And he takes this to mean something.

"Are you suggesting we cut her breasts off, when she gets them?" I asked.

"No, no. Much simpler. We remove the buds."

"There are buds?"

"They look like little almonds," he said, "and without them, she remains flat and safe. Nothing grows without a seed." Dr. Keller rolled on, his voice raised up in a smile. "We can solve another problem too. If we put her on enough hormones, her bones will fuse. We can freeze her at her current size. She'll always fit in your arms."

There were more stories here, of children whose minds are like infants' but whose bodies grow to two hundred and fifty pounds. Who beat their parents with plates. Whose fists are the size of watermelons. Who

have to live in padded rooms and see their mothers
only through shatterproof glass.

"So we freeze her, cut out the seeds where breasts
come from and take away her womb? Is this all in one
day?" Roger asked.

"The hormones are ongoing. The rest takes an hour,
plus overnight in the hospital, plus recovery at home."

When we hung up the phone, I went into your
room and shook your hand. I wanted to congratulate
you on your optimism. Poppy, your body is going about
its business. Blood gets where it needs to. All the pieces
are intact, at least for now. Your body seems to see no
reason not to go forward. To make ready for new life.

I took the bosses on the tour after the rewrite and the new lights
and effects, and they were overcome with joy. They were clinging to each other, at least for fun, when we went down to the
old Art Deco first-class swimming pool with its light-green tile
dressed up nicely with fake mildew.

"Staff have reported seeing the footprints of a child around
the pool," I told them. "And no matter how many times we mop
the thing dry, it's always wet in the morning." I raised my eyebrows and waited for the hologram of a white-dressed girl to
float by.

After that we descended to the boiler room, huge and black,
still full of machine parts and metal tubing, the walkways
sailors used. I told them how those men died when something
blew. Steamed to death. Pretty soon the lights started to flash
and fake steam shot out of a fake engine. The lights went red

and then off. "When thousands of soldiers lived on this ship during the war, there was a terrible wreck. Hundreds of men were crushed or drowned in the icy waters. Others were likely burned to death. They say that the ghosts of all those men live right here in the bow of the *Queen*, waiting for revenge." After exactly two seconds, the "bolts" suddenly started to loosen and streams of water flooded in.

The bosses talked about the end of the bankruptcy and certainly the end of the historical tour upstairs. They shook my hand. "Whatever we're paying you isn't enough," one suited woman told me.

"Yes," I answered.

I looked around for the real ghosts, who did not reveal themselves to me. I imagined them watching us from their endlessness, waiting for us to imitate them and their deaths over and over for paying customers who go upstairs afterward and order lunch at the restaurant looking out over the bow, pretending it's 1930 and they are on their way to England in fancy dresses and smooth black suits. They pour packets of sugar into their glasses and then suck the drink out with a straw. Human things, living things, things no one ever puts on a list of what to be grateful for.

Dear Poppy,

 This morning we sat together on the porch. It was warm enough to be without jackets for the first time this spring. You were in your chair, which I want to tell you is made of a stroller meant for twins. We have turned the seats to face each other and they are reclined. There is a full sheepskin for your mattress. It was your father who made it. There are some devices marketed for kids like you. They are covered in buttons and levers and look like they will take you nowhere but white rooms full of more buttons and levers. Your father wanted to make something himself that was just yours, not a bed for severely disabled children, of which you are one, but a bed for his daughter, Poppy, who needs one with wheels. Anyway, you like it and you are in it a lot.

We were out there on the porch and I put some seed in the bird feeder and we waited for something to come and eat it. I told you about the birds we have here: mostly sparrows and crows but sometimes goldfinches and robins. I told you how they do not make babies the way we do but they lay eggs and inside the eggs the babies grow until they peck their way out. I felt stupid saying this out loud. I know that you do not store up the knowledge I give you. I know that I am repeating to myself the most basic facts about this world. It is only one of many humiliations. Another is how I write these letters to you when you are right next to me. No sound makes its way between our ears. I write as if the scratched words will crawl into your brain and make their nests there to stay for the long haul, stay until you understand them.

Eventually a squirrel came and hung itself from the porch roof by its back feet to eat from the feeder. I thought about getting up to scare it off, it not being *winged. But for a second you seemed to be watching it, so I let it be. It ate up everything in the tray and left the feeder swinging. I did not refill it. You made some of your cooing sounds and the trees answered you with the rustle of their leaves.*

Over lunch I put on an opera recording that always makes you wave your hands around. I am amazed by how little you cry. It does not seem to occur to you. You make sounds and you were fussy about food until we put you on a tube, but you do not seem to feel sadness or do not express it with tears. While you moved your tight fists to the music, I ate a turkey sandwich. I didn't talk to you at all. I read the newspaper and found out about more of the continued misery. I did not do the breakfast dishes or the lunch dishes. I feel I should apologize to you about this—I am not keeping your house well. I am your servant and I am not serving the way I should. But you do not scold me. You wear the clothes I dress you in and do not complain.

IN THE MORNING there was a little girl sitting at my desk. She was watching my small television. I asked, "Are you looking for the ghost tour?"

"I have already been on it. I have done everything on this stupid boat," she said, flipping channels.

"Where are your parents?"

"My dad works the bar upstairs for weddings. Today it's a pink and white theme for Mr. and Mrs. Gravelthorn."

"You have nowhere else to go?"

"It's summer vacation. Don't you have any kids for me to play with?"

"Not like that."

"Can I stay here and draw?"

Before I answered, she set to work. She was surrounded by my life. The pictures of my family. Of Laura standing next to a cactus much taller than she was. Of us together in the car driving east, of Poppy as a baby and one of Poppy as a bigger kid. In this picture she is looking at the camera. I know that it just happened to be where her eyes went, that the flash drew her there, but looking at the picture feels like having her see me. Like she knows everything I want her to.

Dear Poppy,

    When you were born they gave you to me and I loved you. You looked exactly like a baby. My mother said you had my eyes, but I didn't care about that. You had eyes. You had your own face. You opened your mouth and I fed you. Your father's hands were jealous while you nursed. You did not look at our eyes and you still don't.

    It took several weeks before they could tell us with any certainty that you would not grow up right. I hate remembering us then. We believed all day long that we could save you. We called experts all over the country. We drove you around in the car, me sitting next to you in back, singing, and your father steering us along. My mother flew in and stayed. People had answers for us, things to try, whole visions of how your life might turn out, you walking the stairs at the end of the school day with a heavy bag of books. Us a regular family. I can't remember if there was a day when I changed the story, knowing you would lie where I placed you and stay there, your arms waving around and nothing I could understand going through your mind.

I mentioned to Dr. Keller that I was writing you letters lately, before the surgery, trying to explain your life to you. He told me that he wrote to both of his sons before their circumcisions. How he wanted to explain his reason for cutting them like that, the lineage of Jewish men they would be joining. He paused afterward, realizing, I think, that my letters were not the same thing. You will never read them. There will not be another ceremonial coming-of-age where I find you old enough to take you behind the dark stage of your life and show you the ropes and pulleys, show you the clanking steel and the costume room, and then the two of us reenter holding hands and the theater is full and we take a long mother-daughter bow and you go on being a woman after that. In this case, the letters remain in the box. I show them to no one. And you go on.

On the first tour, two kids got scared and had to be taken back by Britney, whose job it is to follow us along and remove anyone who is freaking out. There was only one couple left after that. It is much harder to lead a small tour, because you don't get the group fear going. It's just me, this dopey guide, acting afraid for the hundredth time. The husband was not interested at all in ghosts or in effects.

When the lights went out and the fake steam started to howl from the "broken" pipeline, the guy says to me, "So, like how many men would be working down here at a time, say?"

I tried to ignore him but he persisted, so I told him hundreds of thousands. The lights flickered on and off and the recorded sounds of screaming men echoed in the metal cavern. His wife seemed slightly frightened but never said anything during the entire tour.

"Now, were they *unionized?*"

"Are you kidding me? Do you know what my job is?" I asked him. "My job is to scare you."

"You don't know how many men it took to build the ship originally, do you?" he called. "You don't know shit! You just make stuff up!"

"My daughter is eight years old and she's growing pubic hair. Does that scare you?"

"You are disgusting. I'm here to see a great ocean liner," he said. "A *historic* ocean liner."

I stopped saying anything. I led them through, room by room, signaled the effects and stood quietly while steam and lights and water did their jobs. At the end of the tour, I opened the doors to a fluorescently lit room with a few exhibits of life during the time the ship sailed. Pictures of the now creepy pool filled with happy swim-capped first-classers; a white lace dress such as a lady might have worn to tea in the afternoon. Normally we enter this room and exit right away. For a few minutes then, I can put my feet over the edge and kick them against the curved wood and breathe some actual air and call my wife, who puts the phone to Poppy's ear so I can tell her I miss her. But this guy wanted to stay. This was the part he had been waiting for. He wanted the facts, not the story I wrote for him.

"Oh, look, Marjorie, what a pretty little teaspoon!" he said, and they stood there looking, their old noses pressed up against the glass. By the time they were finally done, there were nose-grease patterns, two dots side by side, on every case. I did not go hunt for Windex and I did not wipe down the cases. Their twin prints remained there, thin and foggy, while I invoked the dead for eighteen minutes on the hour and the half hour for the rest of the day.

> *Dear Poppy,*
>
> *I wanted to buy something to wear to the surgery tomorrow. I want them to believe me, that I'm doing my best. If I arrive looking how I do most of the time, I think they'll do less of a job for you. They need to think that we are the kind of family who demands good service. We rolled through the awful mall looking at pantsuits. I held them over you so you could see, but you were no help. When I tried them on, I looked like someone I would not like to be friends with. I bought a boring blue turtleneck sweater, but at least it's clean. As we left the mall, in the central food court there was a little girl about three years old with gold curls bouncing on her shoulders, running ahead of her parents, who seemed entirely unbothered, yelling, "I'm African! I'm*

*African! I'm African! I'm African!" In her mind, was
she riding on the back of a zebra over a stretch of
land so vast it would be days before she encountered
someone who corrected her story, made her put her
seat belt on, bribed her to eat six more bites of potatoes
before dessert?*

*We went to the grocery store in the afternoon. I
decided that I wanted to make a nice supper for us all.
I chose a cart over a basket and made my way around
the store with two sets of wheels, yours and the food's.
I chose lamb chops and the makings for salad. I put
four red potatoes into a bag. I still think it's weird to
cook for only two. You do not ever, not ever, eat what
I make. I think you are ungrateful sometimes. I think
you do not even see what I do. You laugh and smile
while I stir and chop. You laugh and smile while I
measure your medicines and attach a new bag of
food for you. You laugh and smile while I clean you.*

*An old lady in the cereal aisle stared up at me with
my two vehicles. She looked into your bed and waited
for me to pull you over so that she could pass.*

"You are a saint," she said to me.

*"What am I supposed to do?" I asked back. "Take
her outside and shoot her?"*

*Usually I am practiced at saying, "Thank you for
saying so, but it's no burden. She is always a blessing."
And this is not untrue. I imagine you gone and it seems
horribly empty. I imagine the games of healthy children*

in the living room and the children seem like loud and insulting beasts. "I don't mean that," I told the old woman. "She is always a blessing." She seemed to accept this, eager, too, to pave over my indiscretion. She wants this to be a place where God sends down the questions of twisted bodies and damaged brains but always sends with them the answers of wide hearts and abundant love.

In the parking lot, a bird flew over us with a fish in his claws. They were about the same size. The fish faced forward and flapped its tail. It flew. It swam through the air. What a surprise that must have been, to be swimming along and then suddenly to be plucked out and held between the sharp talons of a hawk, swooping out over the hills. Suffocating in all that air.

The girl was still in my chair when I got back at the end of the day. She was watching TV.

"So," I said.

"Hello."

"You're still here."

"My name is Madeleine. I'm eight." She smiled, sharp. "You?"

"OK. Roger. I'm forty-three. Almost forty-four." I kept talking. I did not find a stopping place. "My birthday is in May. The fifteenth. The ides of May." I laughed in hollow, uncomfortable rounds. She nodded politely.

"Happy early birthday. I finished my drawing." She took the paper out. It was Poppy, from the photograph. She looked upsettingly happy in it, the kind of happy where she can tell you exactly how the good things went down—the soccer goal, the A on the math test, the birthday gifts opened and piled.

"You drew my daughter."

"I know."

"What's it called?"

"I don't know. How about *Still Life with Child*." She gave it to me and I folded it up and put it in my pocket.

"*Still Life with My Child*," I repeated. "We can't be friends, me and you."

"OK. Why?"

"I already have a kid."

"I know—I drew her. And I already have a dad. I just wanted to use your desk."

When I got home, my girls were asleep on the couch. Poppy was covered in a hand-knit blanket and Laura was uncovered, open to the world. Her pants were twisted around her waist and her shirt was falling open, a square of breast visible through the buttonhole. On the floor, Laura's sketchbook was open to a drawing of Poppy's face. Her curled fists were absent. The uneasy shape of her body. In the drawing, her face looked like it could be talked into being normal. A few changed strokes and she would be a regular kid. Oprah was on TV without sound. She sat on her white couch and laughed with a famous person. They looked serious for a moment and then they rejoiced. Serious, rejoice, serious, rejoice. I could hear the breathing of my wife and daughter above all else. They were not in sync. I sat in the nearby chair and did not change anything.

Dear Poppy,

My mother was the last to admit your differences. She came to stay here from Boston when you were born and knit about a hundred blankets and hats and booties. She cooked us dinner every night and changed diapers and sang to you and me and everyone else. She was making a loud entrance as a grandmother. I saw that she had been waiting. When we first learned that you might not develop normally, she went on a tirade about the incompetence of doctors. "They always want to give you a prognosis," she told me. "It's a baby! How do they know anything about what's going to happen!"

"They aren't predicting that she'll be a pro ice skater or that she'll fail the seventh grade. They are taking note of her functioning, her body's functioning."

"Of course they are. And who stands to gain from that? How many tests do they want to conduct now? And what's the price of those tests?"

"Should I refuse them, then?"

"You tell me that there is something wrong with your daughter. Say it, then, if you think it's true. Say, 'My daughter is a retard.'"

I didn't say anything to her. I did let them do tests, though, and they kept coming back with bad news. Even still, your grandmother was your big fan all along. She was the one who set up most of our appointments with learning specialists and everyone else. These people told us happily in their

*offices that everyone has a different way of developing
and all we'd have to do was embrace yours.*

*She visits you every three months. She still
looks at you like a healthy girl. Your uncle has two
now, so Grandma gets to do the regular things, which is
good for her. She plays softball and reads Tintin to
them. But when she comes here, she sits right down
next to you and rubs your arms while she tells you
about the world. "There have been some big trades in
baseball already this year," she says, "and I don't
know if you know, but I think the political tide might
finally be turning." You seem to listen. Your eyes are
alert and you squeeze her hand back as if to say, "I
hear you."*

We ate outside. It has not been warm enough in months, and we
wore our coats and wool socks. Laura put out a nice tablecloth
and we forked lamb and potatoes into our mouths with the
sound of wind shaking the trees out. There were no buds yet,
but the trees seemed ready. They seemed to be putting their
fingers up, considering when to unroll this year's greenery.

"How you doing, Poppy girl?" I said to her, holding her
hand. Her eyes were bright but did not meet mine. "You had a
good day?" I waved her hand around, I kissed each of her fingers. "Today I scared a lot of people—aren't you proud?"

"She sang a lot," Laura told me. "We sat out here all afternoon and she sang back to the birds. A squirrel came and ate the
birdseed. I didn't stop it."

"A singing lady? That's you?"

I do not know how to talk to my daughter in any way but as to a baby. She is the size of a large dog now. Her hands are hands, not miniatures, but my voice still jumps an octave when I address her. Laura is better about this. Though she lifts Poppy out of bed to bathe her, though she sits at the side of the tub and washes, she does not baby talk.

I heard her say through the bathroom door this morning, in the same, even voice she uses to speak to me, "You are covered in shit, my love."

Poppy's room is next to ours, and a door has been installed to connect them. There is an actual door, but for us what matters is the hole in the wall. Poppy's bed has rails on it so that she doesn't scoot herself out in the night. She sleeps the way she lives—on her back. Her entire world consists of whatever is above her. The nubby ceiling is her vista. Her panorama.

In our bed, Laura and I move close. She used to sleep naked and I remember the feeling of our skins wrapped up. Now she likes to be ready to jump out of bed and take care. To wash and comfort.

"There was a girl in my office today," I whispered. "Someone else's kid." I waited for her to be angry.

"Are you trying to admit something to me?"

"I don't know. She drew Poppy."

"So did I."

"I saw—it's nice. A nice drawing."

"Of a nice daughter," she said. "What about this girl?"

"Poppy will never get to sit in my office chair and draw. It doesn't seem fair that some other kid can."

Laura laughed and brushed her hand over my neck. "You

don't have to avoid contact with every other child on earth. Poppy doesn't care who sits in your chair, Roger. Poppy doesn't even know your name."

Around us the room was full of its noises. The streetlight outside went off for a second and then flashed back on.

Dear Poppy,

There was another letter addressed to us today, forwarded from the doctor. Since he gave a presentation about his planned procedure on you at a medical conference, he's been getting a lot of mail, which he seems to want us to see. I don't know if he is proving a commitment to his convictions or hoping that we'll reconsider and save us all. It was postmarked from Lincoln, Nebraska. I opened it before Roger came home but got as far as "You have no right to toy with a body that is not your own" before I put it down. We had been warned.

"There is some concern over the rights of the developmentally disabled" was how the good doctor put it to us.

"Yes, I imagine there is," your father had agreed.

"Of course, we'll have to convince an ethics committee that this is for Poppy's comfort less than our own." I noticed that he was a part of We, part of the fight now, part of the family.

"Are they wrong?" I asked.

"Who?"

"The concerned."

"No. There is a history of euthanasia and medical experimentation. They are not wrong."

"But are they right then?"

He clicked his pen and stood. "I think we in this room know what's good for Poppy," he said, opening the door of his office and standing at it, his arm extended in a polite request for us to leave.

"I don't think we know anything," I said to a fat man stepping on the scale in the hallway.

"We don't know shit," he smiled, shaking his head.

I put the letter on Roger's desk. You and I sat at the kitchen table and I tried to tell you again about what we are saving you from. The horrible cramps. The bleeding. You smiled up at the ceiling. I have stuck a constellation of glow stars above the table because we spend a lot of time here. "And you'd probably inherit my large breasts, which are not even close to what they're cracked up to be."

You shrieked and flapped your flightless arms.

On surgery day, Laura made pancakes before I went to work for the morning. I bathed Poppy like I do on weekends. I turned on the water and got in bed with her while it was running. "How's my girl today?" She cooed and kicked her legs. "You're going to do great, my darling. You are so good, so good, so good." I nuzzled my face into her belly and she approximated a laugh. I think she has a sense of humor.

When the tub was full, I undressed her on her bed and carried her pale form into the bathroom. She loves the water. She goes completely limp. It is as if she is back in the womb, back to try another time, develop better, be born better. I held her head in one hand and washed her with the other. I saw the short hairs that had started us worrying. They could easily have been plucked out and we could have gone on pretending. I saw the tiniest rise in her nipples, standing up now slightly. "Do you wish you could outgrow us? Well, we won't let you." I washed her face with a soapy cloth, moving in careful strokes to avoid her eyes. She blinked and almost looked at me.

Laura had pancakes on the table when we got downstairs. Poppy cannot eat pancakes, as she cannot eat most things. We ate them in her honor though, assuming that an eight-year-old would like them if she could. I poured extra syrup on mine and thought every bite into her mouth.

I went through the tour route turning on the lights and the fog machines and the strobes. When I got to the pool room, I saw Madeleine sitting next to a lying-down man. I moved closer. A rough beard stuck up.

"What the fuck," I whispered.

"His eyes were open but I closed them."

I kneeled down next to them and looked at the man. His skin was blue and his beard was red. His hair poked out in greasy strips.

"Is this a dead person?" I asked, dumb.

"You think?" Madeleine said, mocking. She put his head in her lap. She touched his forehead with her fingertips.

"Don't do that," I said, reaching out to stop her. She pushed my hands away.

"I think his name is Steven. He doesn't like it though and

always wished his name was Rupert. His mother was a seam-stress and his father died when he was very young." She kept smoothing her hands over his face.

"Do you know him?" I asked.

"Of course not. You can be a real jerk. I am telling a story to this guy." Just then, my boss came into the room, laughing.

"You like him?" He smiled. "I had him made. We can rig it so the body floats up in the pool or something. My first idea was to get real bodies in here and try to haunt the place, but the law-yers are assholes."

"You made him?"

"I had him made. He's good, right?" I felt stupid for thinking he was real, stupid for being caught at it.

"This is a ghost tour, not a morgue tour."

"Can I do my job?" Peterson told me. "Can I do that? Your job is to make up a good story about the things I put in front of you. I'd like to introduce you to George, the new fake dead guy. Go find him a nice suit and a pocket watch and give him a life story. Maybe he ended it himself? Maybe his wife held him under so she could run off with some gentleman with not one, but two yachts?"

I stood there quiet.

"You were really scared! Ha! This is going to be a real moneymaker." He walked back out again, clicking his pen and humming the theme to an old TV show.

"This doesn't scare you?" I asked Madeleine.

"He's not real. He's a doll."

I watched her talk. I watched her move her fully functioning hands and adjust her legs and push the hair out of her face.

"What the hell is it like to be a little girl?" I asked her.

"I don't have a lot to compare it to."

"I will give you ten dollars to describe being an eight-year-old."

"Don't you have to go to work?"

"Tell me every single thing," I said, holding a bill out to her.

Dear Poppy,

At the hospital you lay across our laps. You were longer than the bed we made together. Your feet hung. You looked up at my face, reached to it, scratched the bottom of my chin like I was a cat. I purred for you. Roger was reading a magazine with a picture of an actress I've never heard of on the cover. I doubt he had heard of her either. Roger was hunched over to be closer to her, his coat falling off his shoulder and his scarf on the floor. You and I were neighboring planets.

I had my hand on your belly where your womb will not be. You wriggled like a snake. I had this thought: You and I leave, your whole body in my arms. Your father does not notice us go and your stroller stays there too, its various straps hanging toward the floor. We get into the car and drive away. We get pregnant together. Not by men but by sperm. We grow matching stomachs, globes, entire earths of our own. We measure them against each other. We eat the whole aisle of candy and watch movies in bed. Everyone leaves us alone.

When the babies are born, they join us in our bed.

We nurse them together. We hold hands under the covers. The babies learn words. They put the fleshy bundles of their feet on the ground and move over it. They go between us: you on the bed to me on the chair; you on the bed to me standing in the lit doorway; you on the bed to me at the top of the stairs. I feed all three of you with blended foods carried to your mouths on rubber-coated spoons. It is the talking I look forward to most. If you had a child and she could speak to me, then I would be almost speaking to you. If she came from your body, I could ask her, at least, what it was like in there. The slip and bubble, the churning.

We took you into the surgery room and kissed you and kissed you and kissed you before going back to our waiting chairs. In the doorway I turned back and said, "Could we see the breast buds? When you take them out?"

"They look like almonds," the surgeon answered.

"But they aren't almonds. You don't have to show me the uterus. I would please like to see them. Please." He looked at me and shook his head in disbelief.

"Margie will bring them out."

Laura and I crossed half the street to the grass-fuzzy median in front of the hospital. We lay next to each other, the lanes on either side of us quiet, trickling riverbeds.

"Being a kid is OK," I said. "She avoids a lot."

"You don't know what it's like to be her mother."

"Is this a new sweater? It looks nice on you."

"I sort of wish the hormones could shrink her, not just stop her here. I wish she could get so she could fit in my hand. Or smaller."

"Like a doll."

"No chairs, no tubes. Just the two of us."

"The three of us?"

"OK."

She sat up and her spine was a mountain range in her shirt.

"That's what happens when someone dies," I said. "That's when you get to have them everywhere." She nodded, tipped her head to rest on one shoulder.

"There's a lot to look forward to," she said, and began to lie down.

"Wait," I told her, "your hair is full of leaves."

I sat up and started to pull the dry brown pieces out one at a time. They fell apart in my fingers.

Dear Poppy,

We held hands and turned the pages of magazines. We said little. She's going to do great and She's so brave and I love you. I drank more coffee than I should have. It felt like something was about to change, but it wasn't. That was the whole point. We were sending you in there so that nothing would ever change. Your brain has elected to stop where it is, and now your body will be eight years old until one day when you die. Will you get old? Will your hair turn lighter? Will your skin fall wrinkled over your little-girl body?

There was an old man in the waiting room with

a cane and a pair of thick-rimmed glasses that he'd probably had since 1950. He was reading the newspaper and I could see, even from across the room, the sprigs of hair growing out of his ears. I liked him for this. He seemed to be turning into earth, growing grass. I wondered who he was there for. No one joined him all morning and he did not fidget. At around 11:30 a nurse came out and told him, "Your wife did perfectly." He carefully folded the paper up, smoothing it out, and said, "Of course she did."

Another nurse came out holding a small dish with two bloody little beans on it. "These are the breast buds," she told us, sounding bored. "As promised." Before she could stop me, I picked one up and put it in my mouth. "Holy shit," the nurse said, "what the fuck are you doing?" Roger was completely silent. He looked at me, huge eyed and flat faced. "Lady!" the nurse said. "You have to spit that out! That's biohazard! That's not something you can eat!"

I felt the thing in my mouth. It was perfectly smooth. It slipped over the skin of my cheek and my tongue. I could feel the threads of veins.

"Ma'am. Lady. You have to spit that out immediately." She turned and looked around for someone who could help her. The desk was nurseless. No blue-scrubbed person in sight.

Roger put his hand on my back. "Maybe you should spit it out, Laura."

"Too late. I swallowed it."

"Holy shit!" the nurse says, "Jesus. Lady."

But, Poppy, as the nurse was turning, spinning on her heels, looking for a kind of help she had never needed before, your father plucked the other bud out of the dish and held it in his hand. He looked at me and his lips spread out in a smile. The nurse looked into the glass dish smeared with a little pink blood. She shook her head and then suddenly she went quiet. She stopped her search and whispered to us, "You all are fucking nuts. Please don't tell anyone this happened." And off she went with her empty dish.

We ran outside holding hands. I spit the breast bud out into my palm.

"I thought you swallowed it," he said.

I shook my head. "I had to lie so she'd let me go. Come on." In the median I knelt down and began to dig a hole. Your father understood right away and helped, his left hand a protective fist, his right a shovel. In a few minutes, we had come to darker soil and we both put the seeds of you inside, covered them in earth. "To growing," I said. "Whatever that might mean." We sat down and held hands. We did not look at each other, but we squeezed our fingers tight together. Both of our cheeks were streaked from crying.

Inside, the doctors sewed the openings up with thread, your chest safely sealed in immaturity. The two of us held on to each other while, in the darkness of the earth, your unbloomed seeds were at rest.

GESTATION

Atria

HAZEL WHITING had finished her freshman year at Mountain Hills High, where there were a lot of ponytails and a lot of clanging metal lockers with pictures of hotties taped inside. She had some friends there but not too many and would usually rather be by herself than discussing other people's haircuts or dreamed-of love lives. The truth of those love lives—a glance in the dingy hallway from a crushable boy, a dark tangled session on an out-of-town parent's couch—was like a tiny, yellowed lost tooth, hidden under a pillow, which the high-schoolers believed, prayed, would be soon replaced by gorgeous, naked, adoring treasure.

Hazel, of course, wanted love some day too, and she did admit to feeling a whir in her chest when she thought about a bed shared with a boy—or a man, by then. Still, when she looked at Bobbie Cauligan's gelled-back hair and calculated leather jackets, or the white, always-new sneakers and tennis-club polos strutted by Archer Tate, or the billowing, too-big flannel shirts of the shy boys like Russel Fieldberg-Morris and Duncan

Story as they tried to dart from the safety of one classroom to another, Hazel did not see the possibility of love. *Will these people look more like humans when they are grown?* she thought. Now they looked to Hazel like children, like beasts, like helpless, hairless baby rats. *Do I look like that to them too?* she wondered. Whatever it was, high school was a soggy thing, being a teenager was a soggy thing, and Hazel had decided early on in each of these endeavors that she would survive by not becoming invested.

Hazel chose not to follow the troupes of other girls toward endless slumber parties and pictures of models torn from magazines stuck to mirrors in order that they would be reminded every morning, while popping a pimple or switching the part in their hair, of the distance between beauty and their own unfinished faces. Instead, Hazel wanted to walk and observe the day as it revealed itself unspectacularly around her. She wanted the feeling that her life was a small thread in the huge tangle of the world and that nothing she did one way or another mattered all that much.

The last week of May, while her mother held meetings about the potholes and the winter food-drive, Hazel walked all over town, street by street. She upped one block and downed the next while ladies watered their white roses and the few men home during the day—retired or sick or broke—sat in the window reading the paper. When Hazel returned for a sandwich in the middle of the day, she found her mother in their newly renovated blue and yellow kitchen, bent over the construction of a low-this high-that salad, trying feverishly to grate an almond. "Why are you doing that?" Hazel asked.

"The body has an easier time breaking down foods that aren't whole," her mother answered, scraping the single nut.

"What's the point of breaking something if it isn't whole?" Hazel asked. Her mother looked up at her and narrowed her eyes in a comic-book glare.

"You are such a teenager," she said. "I felt done with this stage after your sisters went through it, and that was ages ago. Now I'm right back where I started. Couldn't you just skip ahead?"

"Gladly."

While she kicked a rock down the oak-lined streets, Hazel considered her mother's wish. Perhaps, if she opened her arms to whatever came, stopped turning it all away, she might arrive at adulthood earlier. Adulthood was a place Hazel always pictured as a small apartment kitchen far away from anyone to whom she was related, furnished with upturned milk crates and exactly one full place setting.

After a lot of afternoon walking Hazel wanted a break and a snack or a soda with a straw. She went to the 7-11, where she always sat out back on a nice bit of grass that was close enough to the dumpsters so no one else came, but far enough away that she didn't smell anything except when there was a big gust or a bad bag.

JOHNNY WAS TO BE HER FIRST. He came out of the store on his lunch break, his uniform button-down untucked, planning to piss on the trash bins because they were cleaner than the toilets. He was clearly surprised to see a girl there, but he just said hello and paused for a second before going on with his plan anyway. Johnny stood with his back to her, a plastic bag in his left hand and his right hidden. She could hear two things: him whistling "Strangers in the Night," and a delicate stream hitting the green metal of the dumpster. After, he sat down next to Hazel and took a large package of teriyaki beef jerky and a six-pack of Miller Lite out of his bag.

He started right in about the horse races in Deerfield and the off-track betting down in Green Springs. He told her about Million Dollar Mama and Sweet Sixteen, both winners. But not Johnny, he'd lost fifty. "Just not my lucky day," he said. When he said "lucky day," he looked right into Hazel's eyes and winked, and it looked as if he'd been practicing for years in his rearview. She sucked her lemon-lime fizzy and noticed his arms, skinny and brown like hungry snakes.

Just a few feet behind where Hazel and Johnny had talked, they lay down on their young backs. There was a muddle of bushes there, hiding them from the road and the midday gassers and snackers. Johnny didn't have a line, had just asked, "Wanna go lie down behind those bushes?"

"OK," Hazel said, because she did not have a better answer, and because, having decided the hour before to say yes to growing, she could hardly say no.

He carried her soda for her, left his two empties where they were. When she sat, he said, "Nice hair."

"Thanks."

He leaned over and kissed her, putting his tongue right into the center of her mouth and moving it around in whirling circles. It tasted like beef jerky and beer. She decided she was supposed to do the same—two tongues spinning now. But then she wanted a rest, pulled her head back. Johnny took the pause to mean: OK, next step. He rolled on top. He moved his hips the same way he'd moved his mouth. She could feel him pressed into her bladder.

Hazel had had one close call before, in eighth grade with a pimply boy named Derek who was the brother of the girl having the slumber party. Everyone else had fallen asleep and they had made out in the laundry room while the other girls slept to the sound of *Texas Chainsaw Massacre*. Screaming sounds masked the washing machine's rattle as Hazel and Derek pressed themselves together on top of a pile of mateless socks.

Johnny got the courage to grab her breasts. He sat up, straddling her, and put one big hand on each B-cup. Squeezed, pumped like udders. He did not softly caress and he did not pinch. Just squeezed and released, squeezed and released. She could tell this was making him happy because his closed eyes were squinting and his mouth was pursed up. *Mmmmmm*, he said. *Mmmmm*, she returned. Hazel thought they were like whales in the sea, searching for something over long, dark distances.

Johnny took his shirt off and her shirt off. He had a few scratchy little hairs. Then pants and pants. He looked at her and said, "OK?" She didn't know exactly what he meant, but she nodded. She found out right away that it meant underwear, and in a second they were both off—his first, then hers. He rolled on top, ungraceful and floppy, bit his lower lip and pushed. Hazel started out making her noise but then realized he didn't notice either way, so she stopped and instead watched his big head lit up by the sun. *This is it?* she thought. *This is the whole entire thing?*

Hazel went home that night and ate salad with her mother on the screened-in porch while the mosquitoes tapped audibly to get in. Hazel lived alone with her mother, though she had three sisters, all much older, all living in their own houses with their own dishwashers, lists of emergency phone numbers, and husbands who had good jobs, good values and well-shaped eyebrows. This family had been symmetrical, a family of plans and lists and decisions made years in advance into which Hazel was a very late, very surprising accident followed almost immediately by her father's diagnosis. While Mother grew fatter, Father grew smaller, and everyone felt certain that they were watching a direct transfer of life from one body to another.

The two of them were never in the world together—by the time Hazel entered, her father had already closed the door behind him. Her mother was still wearing black in the delivery room, surrounded by a ring of grieving daughters. The final shock came when the baby was a not a boy but a girl, looking nothing like the man she was meant to replace.

"How was your afternoon?" Hazel's mother asked.

"Fine," Hazel said, considering if this was a true answer and deciding it was. "Yours?"

"Just the usual disasters. The club has the red, white and blue flowers ordered in time for the Fourth, and what is the city out there planting in every median? Marigolds."

Hazel did not tell her mother that she had had sex with a convenience-store clerk and that it was disappointing but harmless—she felt no ache to see the boy again, no real change in her own body, no broken heart. She had done this grown-up thing, yet she knew her mother would find her even more child-ish for it.

HAZEL WALKED the northern quadrant of town and, since it was a Saturday, there were a lot of folks out in their yards trim-ming bushes and pulling dandelions out of the ground with flowered-canvas hands. The day after that, it was the same thing, only the western quadrant, where she watched the first few innings of a family softball game and petted some dogs in the dog park. She walked past a flower shop where the dyed-blue carnations were the best thing going. She walked through the church parking lot. Father O'Donnel's Honda was the only car there. She peeked into the backseat: an open gym bag, one ratty gray running shoe out, one in.

"Hi," someone said roughly. Hazel turned around fast. It was a tall man and big, too. He had a fat face and a comb-over; his shirt buttons were barely holding. He was close.

"Hi," she said.

"Hi," he said again. She edged to her right, her back pressed up against the car.

"Are you hungry?" he asked.

"No. Thanks." Hazel tried to smile.

"Oh. I'd like to talk to you."

"I have to go."

"Actually, you have to stay." He put his hand on her arm, but didn't grab hard. She didn't say anything, wanted to play it smart. "Look," he said, "don't scream. I won't hurt you if you don't scream." Hazel did not scream. Later she thought she might have been better off if she had. But at that moment everything was underwater and she was underwater and there was a strong current pulling her deeper.

The big-faced man took her hand, almost gently. His round fingers interlaced with her skinny ones. Her heart took over her entire body. She was a drum. Did she ask the obvious questions? *Why am I walking? Why am I not drinking a Shirley Temple and adjusting my bikini top over and over at the country-club pool like all the other girls? Why did I agree to grow up?* Her body asked the questions for her, that terrified, slamming heart spoke them so loud that she could not breathe fast enough to fuel it, but the drumbeat was empty of answers. They walked behind the church, under the dark of the steeple-shaped shadow and into the maples covered in the new green of summer leaves. The man stopped walking and smiled at her.

"I just want to have some sex with you," he said. "I won't hurt you if you have some sex with me." She was barely breathing, the trees were barely breathing, and the turned earth from their footsteps smelled cold. Hazel thought about running or screaming or kicking, but she just looked up at him and said, "Please. Wait. Help."

He pulled her down to the ground and he kissed her neck. He undid pants and pants. His breath, strong and bitter with alcohol, was boiling water on her face. His mouth was right up next to her mouth but he didn't kiss her, just breathed into her. She turned her head but he followed. She could not avoid his lungy air. His weight was everywhere. Two words kept pinging in her mind, though she did not know what they meant. *And yet, and yet, and yet.*

A TINY WHITE SPINE began to knit itself inside Hazel. Now it was just a matter of growing. Hazel sat on the closed toilet next to a little plastic spear with a bright blue plus sign on one end. She put her hands in her hair, tried to hold her head up.

She thought of the men that could have created this. "How could you be a real living thing?" she asked her growing baby. "How could you be a person?" She dreamed that night, and for all the nights of summer, of a ball of light in her belly. A glowing knot of illuminated strands, heat breaking away from it, warming her from the inside out. Then it grew fur, but still shone. Pretty soon she saw its claws and its teeth, long and yellow. It had no eyes, just blindly scratched around sniffing her warm cave. She did not know if this creature was here to be her friend or to punish her.

"MOTHER," Hazel said in the kitchen in early fall where the difficult process of roasting a duck was under way. Hazel's mother was holding it by the neck over a large pan, searing.

"Yes, darling," her mother said.

"I need to tell you something."

"My wallet is in the front hall. I, for one, would like to see you in a pair of decent shoes."

"I am very pregnant." Hazel's fear had so far been sitting, quietly twirling his cane and reading how-to manuals, waiting for Hazel to acknowledge him there.

The duck dropped to the pan.

Hazel omitted Johnny and the 7-11 from her story. She omitted her own fault from the story, she omitted any possibility of a father. Hazel's mother looked up at her with every kind of lost in her eyes. She lifted up the baggy sweatshirt Hazel had on and looked at her belly and started to cry. "Who was he? How could he do that to you?" And then quickly, "*I will take care of everything.*" The cane twirler twirled his cane and tapped his shiny shoes together. He winked at Hazel from under a top hat, saying with his big eyes, *There is so much now that you have to hold on to.*

Hazel's mother began her crusade. The police came and took a description, drew a man who looked nothing like anyone Hazel had ever seen. The drawing was pinned to each lamppost in town until it rained and the posters shredded and bled, leaving torn bits of paper all over the sidewalk. A women's self-defense class got started up at the gym. The mayor proposed a citywide emergency phone system in Hazel's name. But Hazel herself was not meant to benefit from any of these activities. Too late now for self-defense, too late to find a bright yellow phone with a direct line to the police. School started back up and she went, stared at and eyed and gossiped about, and then she walked home, where her sisters came over in shifts, bringing her movies and trays of Poor-Hazel Cookies.

.   .   .

FOR THE TOWN, in a way, it was exciting to have an Illegitimate Bastard Baby from a Rape, because people had plenty to talk about and plenty of sympathy to dispatch. People whispered in the grocery store aisles, "Did you hear about that poor Whiting girl behind the church? And to think the Lord was right next door. I'm going to drop off a casserole later."

If you could have lopped off all the pointed roofs of all the yellow-white houses and watched from above, you would have seen the top of a blond head in each kitchen, pulling hot pans out of the oven, steam rising off meat loaves and lasagnas, the counter covered in empty tuna cans, the severed heads of zuc-chini lying in heaps. A line of station wagons streamed past the Whitings', reheatables meant to make their way from Ford and Dodge right into the stomachs of the grieving. Hazel's mother stopped answering their door after a while. Their freezer was full, their refrigerator and mini garage refrigerator were full. Casserole dishes started to pile up on the front steps. Baked ziti baked again in the sun. Beth Berther, who could not cook even one thing, left a grocery-store cake—chocolate with chocolate frosting and the word *Condolences!* scrawled in orange cursive on top.

People also started to deliver diaper bags and bouncy swings and little hats made to look like various vegetables. Hazel wrote thank-you notes and felt bad that her strange fur baby would be unable to wear the woolen gifts. She saved them in a box under her bed, the bed where she stayed most of the time when she was not in school. Where she was when her mother came in every morning with lemon tea and a biscuit. Where her mother sat, her big reddish-blond hair full of light, singing "Go Tell It on the Mountain" until the breakfast tray was empty and she'd leave singing "Jesus Christ is born," as she closed the door behind her.

BY MONTH SIX, the glowing ball-baby had turned itself into a large bird of prey. It spread and curled its wings. Hazel felt them strong and tickling. The nest it was building was a round of borrowed organs, her small intestine twisted up in a pink knot, the bird's sharp claws resting in the center. Then the bird started to lay eggs, white and the size of a fist. Hazel bought yarn and began to knit three-pronged booties, which she had to invent a pattern for. She planned sweaters with wing holes. She hummed the blues.

Soon Hazel felt the eggs starting to hatch. They cracked and tiny beaks worked to break the surface of the shell, milky eyes and wet feathers emerging into the warm pinkness. The mother bird cuddled them under her wings. She fed them Hazel's digested meals through her beak. The babies twittered and grew. There were too many though, and as their bodies got larger they couldn't move anymore. They were packed in, their famously good eyes useless now, pressed up against the walls of the cave.

Meanwhile, school was exactly as boring as it had always been. Hazel was smiled at more because she was frowned at more. "My mother says God is glad you are keeping the innocent baby," a senior said to Hazel at her locker. "And I don't agree that being raped makes you a slut." The girl handed her a piece of notebook paper with a list of names on it. In the girl column: Grace, Honor, Constance, Mary, Faith. And in the boy column: Peter, Adam, David, Axl Rose.

Hazel thought about a giant bird of prey with the name Constance.

The birds couldn't open their womb-smashed beaks to eat and they began to starve to death. Hazel could feel them getting weaker. They made no noise; they didn't twitch or flutter. One morning she woke up and knew they were dead. Knew their bodies had given up and were now just a mess of needle-bones and feathers. Hazel cried in the shower while she washed herself with Dove. For weeks she could feel the empty weight of them in her. She tucked the booties in the back of her underwear drawer. Through the end of fall and into winter, the avian bodies stayed. Snow was outside on the ground and storms were inside Hazel as the bodies started to flake like ash, layer after layer turned gray and fell. The pile was frozen inside the windless space.

Before Thanksgiving break, the girls and boys were separated and shown charts of each other's bodies. They learned that chlamydia was not a pretty blossom to add to a floral arrangement. The girls, not the boys, were each given a sack of flour with a smiley face drawn on it that they had to carry around and feed with a dry bottle. "Hazel doesn't have to do this assignment," the teacher said to the class. "We all know why." The girls gathered in the bathroom and changed the white-dusted diapers. Some bought little outfits for their flour babies—cute dresses and hats and bows. The teacher pulled them all back into the classroom, where a large penis sat erect on her desk, and said, "These are not dolls, ladies. You aren't supposed to be having fun with this exercise."

The pile of ashes turned into something else. Hazel couldn't tell what it was at first, but knew that it had little round hooves. Night by night it got clearer. The body and the long legs, and then it started to grow three heads, distinctly giraffelike. The necks lengthened, limp poles loosely twisted together like bread dough, with heads bobbing at their skinny ends.

Hazel spent the weekend in bed. She pulled her yellow-and-orange-flowered quilt up to her chin and lay on her back.

Mother said, "Maybe Father will finally come back," patting her daughter's rounded belly.

"If I'm not him, I don't think my baby will be either," Hazel said. Her mother's eyes looked desperate, so Hazel added, "Maybe he will." Her sisters came to sit with her, circled their hands over her pregnantness. One did Hazel's toenails in pink polish, and one rubbed her hands with rose oil. One washed her hair in the sink, braided it into two damp plaits.

One night, the giraffe flipped itself upside down just like that, a perfect blue-mat somersault. Two short ears flicked, and head number one began to emerge. Hazel was so surprised she didn't figure out what was going on until the head was already out. The neck though, she felt all of that, not painful but strange and slithery. Inch by inch by inch, it came. It unfurled. The giraffe blinked and smiled right at her. It bent its head around and came nose to nose with Hazel and sniffed her. Necks number two and three also exited her body.

The giraffe heads rolled out their three long purple tongues and licked Hazel's chest. Cleaned her arms and her face. The tongues were rough and ragged and she shone with their spit, her chest paint-white and glistening. They slept there, breathing softly, their lips quivering. The giraffe's body never came out. It stayed curled up, rising and falling with the inhales of its own three heads and the inhales of its beautiful host.

In the morning, Hazel still had the markings on her breasts from fur pressed down. She could still smell their warm skin like hay and cheese.

HAZEL WENT TO THE DOCTOR for her usual checkup.

"You have a beautiful cervix," he said. Hazel, staring up at the poster on the ceiling of a coral reef, said, "Thank you. I get that all the time." Dr. F laughed so long, all the time still staring into her, that she wished she hadn't said anything at all.

The doctor retrieved Hazel's mother for the dressed part of the exam. He had the picture from the ultrasound in his hand, a gray, curled blob. Hazel didn't want to see it, and didn't believe it when she did. *What a good disguise my baby has on*, she thought. Dr. F rubbed goo on her belly and listened. Her skin was stretched so far it was unrecognizable, not forgiving and soft but stiff and hard.

Hazel's mother stood up from her plastic chair and took a listen. She immediately started to cry and stood there, eyes wide and slippery, her hand on her chest. While her mother witnessed the miracle of life, Hazel rolled the corner of her paper gown in her fingers.

. . .

HAZEL'S MOTHER TALKED about cribs and carriages and binkies and diapers. She insisted on stopping at Babies"R"Us to stock up. Hazel waited in the car and listened to the Soft Rock Less Talk station but turned it off when the host started making jokes about his wife's credit card bill. She watched people pull into the parking lot in minivans and unload kid after kid crying, screaming or jumping around. Mothers struggled to strap them into strollers, to get shoes on and tied. One mother, after a long fight to get her son into his sweatshirt, spit into her delicate, diamond-glittering hand and smoothed it over his parted blond hair.

Hazel's mother thundered back with her full cart, its metal vibrating loudly over the asphalt. She unloaded boxes and bags into the backseat, tossed Hazel a pair of miniature soft orange booties that looked like tennis shoes complete with plush tread and real laces. Hazel stuck her first two fingers into each one, walked them across the dashboard. "If it has four legs, I guess we can just get another pair," she said quietly.

Her mother was busy stuffing the full bags in and shaking the right key out. "It's not twins—we would have seen it in the pictures."

"I never said it was twins."

WITH HER MOTHER OUT one weekend morning, Hazel walked very slowly and heavily to the 7-11. She picked out a six-pack of

Miller and a bag of beef jerky. Johnny, behind the counter, said, "I heard what happened."

"I'm sorry," she told him.

"Do you need anything?" he asked.

"People are being helpful. Do you sell ribbon?"

"I don't really know, but I think you're not supposed to be drinking. You know, in your condition," Johnny said, pulling out a roll of red. Hazel paid for her items and then, standing there with Johnny, she tied the beer and jerky together with the ribbon.

"Here," she said, "it's for you. I hope you understand." She went out the door, which rang its bell to say, *Goodbye, whoever you are.*

With one week to go till due date, Hazel stopped sleeping. She couldn't keep her eyes shut or her mind shut. Her brain bled a list of worries, ongoing and impossible to ignore. All the things she had to remember to do as a mother. She started lists, animal by animal.

Lion: lie under a tree together with its tail wrapped around my leg, learn to cook its caught rabbits, braid its mane. Koala: grow eucalyptus, watch it climb trees, lie underneath looking up at it through the branches. She had stacks and stacks of these lists. Some animals were blank. She didn't know yet how to care for a sloth or a platypus. Almost as an afterthought, she made a list called Human Baby: hire a math tutor, record enough home video but not too much, bake lemon meringue pies, move to a remote unpopulated island when he/she turns thirteen, sled.

. . .

THEY NUMBED HAZEL from the waist down for the birth. It took a few minutes before it started to work, but then Hazel felt the warm emptiness creep over her. She could feel her body melting away. She held her mother's hand. Her sisters wore sweat suits and ponytails and looked ready for action, but there wasn't much to do except hope, which they did while they drank thin, fake-creamer coffee out of styrofoam cups.

Hazel's mother fell asleep for a few minutes, her black shirt rolling up to reveal the loose skin of her midriff. The sisters talked of their own offspring and partners. They discussed a spinach salad recipe from a magazine and a new kind of tea that began in pearls and unfolded into flowers. Hazel could hardly hear them over the sound of her body working to re-lease the creature. All the animals she'd prepared for began to run together. She saw the hooves of a cow and the head of a mouse and the body of a kangaroo. She felt the long teeth of a hyena and the soft fur of an alpaca. Hazel almost felt her own body turn into something else. Something capable of stalking prey and of tearing flesh.

By the time the doctor made the bittersweet announce-ment that this healthy baby was a girl, and all the women in the room gave up hope that their husband and father's sharp fea-tures and smarts would live again, Hazel was lost in her me-nagerie of beasts. She looked right at the bald skin and didn't see it. Didn't believe that the puffy-limbed crier, all pink with bright blue eyes, could be the thing she had been carrying around. Hazel did not reach out when the doctor handed it to her but kept her arms flat by her sides. The baby's body seemed impossible to her, as if she had given birth to a chair or a bicycle.

"It's a nice little girl," the doctor said.

"Whose is it?" Hazel replied. They all laughed warm and low as if she were joking. Her mother took the child from the doctor and rocked her, wrapped her in a pink blanket with big ducks on it. In the growing darkness, Hazel thought a duck's bill might be attached to her child. She fell asleep thinking about it quack quacking around the house with its tail bobbing.

While Hazel was sleeping, Johnny stopped by with three gas-station cloth roses, pink with plastic dew.

"I'm just a friend of Hazel's," he said, leaving the flowers with one of her sisters, who was reading a magazine in the bright hallway.

"You shouldn't bother her," the sister said. "But I'll let her know you stopped by."

"Tell her if she needs anything from the store . . . snacks or whatever. Candy. Smokes. Not that, but you know, I think we sell diapers." The sister brought her eyebrows together and rattled the roses. Johnny's feet were heavy on the floor all the way back down the long corridor. He might have become a father that day, or he might not have. He craved the floating feeling of a moment when everything changes. He wanted to call his mother, tell her the figures: pounds and ounces, inches, exact time of birth, first, middle and last names. None of these were known to him, and his mother would not have understood why she was supposed to care.

. . .

FOUR IN THE MORNING and Hazel was awake. It was raining outside and no one was in the room. Water sheeted and Hazel felt around under the blanket to inspect her body, which was still swollen—a tight, empty globe. What had been growing there was done and out and growing someplace else now. It didn't need her blood or her air.

The room was a dark kind of yellow with a lot of moon and a little hall-light coming under the door. The blinds on the windows chopped the glow into slices and divided Hazel's covered body into slats. She looked around the room at the machines, which breathed back at her. A small red light went on and off. Hoses hung and the shadows of hoses hung lower. A mop and mop bucket. Hazel felt suddenly stuck in a laboratory, caught and studied. She thought she might be left there forever, that her mother had taken her baby and introduced it to the human babies. It would assimilate. It would be accepted into their tribe and given a flowered diaper cover and fed smashed peas. It would never learn to hunt or peck or make its mating call. Hazel sat up and then stood up but got dizzy and sat again. She hit the pillow with her fist.

The baby, who had not been stolen away, but had instead been sleeping in her crib in the corner, began to cry. Hazel got up, slower this time, her pounded and squeezed body creaking as she slid her socks over the linoleum like a skier. There was almost no light in the crib, nothing to brighten the skin of the new life lying there. It cried, the new life. Hazel put her index finger into the crib and poked softly until she felt the warm mound. She touched the ears, the spirals of them. She touched the back of the neck and the front of the neck. She tried to find the mouth, which was still crying. She thought she felt whiskers and a wet nose. She felt soft fur just starting on the top of the head. Suddenly she knew the answer. It was a seal, fat and leg-less. She put her hands over the round eyes, which she knew were black but could not see. The seal barked into her palm and its breath was warm.

This was one animal Hazel hadn't planned for. She thought of the twirling underwater torpedoes in the zoo. It was gill-less, an air breather the same way she was, but it must also like to be wet. She went to the window and opened it, put her hands out in a cup and waited while the air blew cold across her skin. Drops fell but dripped through her fingers and she couldn't collect much. She returned to the flopping baby and rubbed her water-hands onto its face and then its back, which someone had tried to cover with a nightgown, a thing that seemed ridiculous to Hazel.

She remembered the mop bucket and slid her way to it. It was hard to bend down, but she was able to drag it to the crib using the mop as a handle. She pulled the mop up and water streamed down, splashing her feet and the floor. She ran the gray tendrils over the baby, smelling the soap and dirt in the water. It started to cry again. She made shushing sounds in her mouth and tried to hum "Go Tell It on the Mountain." The mop went back and forth, the baby cried, Hazel hummed. She took a deep breath and leaned down to grab the bucket. Sharp shots crossed back and forth in her stomach. She winced and squeezed her eyes shut but kept bending. She caught hold of the handle and lifted. It wasn't as heavy as she had expected, and coming up was easier than going down.

Hazel started to sing the words of the song as she raised the mop bucket over the crib and poured. The water was cold and gray in the dark room. It ran out in ropes, twisting together and splashing into the crib, where the baby cried and threw her small weight back and forth. The blankets soaked through. The thin mattress soaked through. The sleeves of Hazel's nightgown were wet and dripping. The baby's cough was so small it didn't even make it to the walls to bounce.

"Is that enough?" she asked.

No sound came after that, except a dripping *plip plip plip* on the floor. The baby was quiet and Hazel was quiet. The rain continued to be rain, the bed continued to be flat and rumpled. Nurses in other rooms still tried to move soundlessly while they adjusted feeding tubes and emptied bedpans. Hazel's mother was still her mother. Hazel was still not her father and neither was her baby. The two of them would be fatherless together. They would be young together. "Now that I am a mother," Hazel said to the baby, "I get to set the rules. And the rules are: swimming, sunning, playing. Everything else, we ignore." She put the bucket down, empty now, and leaned into the crib to pick up the baby, blanket-wrapped and dripping.

The bundle coughed one beautiful polished river rock of a cough. Hazel put her ear right down against the lips and heard air, in and out. The eyes looked up at her, surprised and afraid. Hazel breathed her air into her baby's mouth and then waited until the baby breathed out so she could inhale that sweetness.

Hazel walked with it around the room, careful and slow.

The body was cool against her. Her clothes stuck to her breasts. She sat down at the edge of her bed. She put the baby down and removed her hospital gown, and then decided to remove the baby's clothes too so their skin could touch. She held the baby to her chest, guided a nipple into the little mouth. Hazel had become aware of the baby's arms and legs, but still saw the seal face, the slick black eyes. She could feel the whiskers brushing against her while it sucked, toothless and quiet.

Chest of Drawers

BEN FELT EMPTY, in the literal sense. He poked at his belly button, at the organs beneath, which were producing no new miracles. As he understood it, his liver was filtering; his gall bladder was storing bile the liver produced during the filtration process; his intestine was connecting the in and the out; and in between, things got broken down with acids. None of that was new. He was the very same machine he had always been.

He followed along with the Miracle of Life by reading books, day-by-day updates of exactly what the spine was doing, what mucus was gathering where. The sacks of air and fluid and the creation of the liver, the urinary tract, the brain. Ben taped pictures of developing fetuses up all over the house. They were on the bulletin board over the dining room table, where receipts and coupons used to go. The black-and-white photographs of soft new heads and still-webbed feet covered the refrigerator. Soon they occupied frames beside the bed, replacing the pictures of friends and parents and vacations. Annie watched her husband remove the evidence of their lived lives in favor of the ghost of their future child. The only remaining photograph of fully formed human beings was of Ben and Annie on their honeymoon, lying in the exact shade of a palm tree, hot white sun inches away from them on every side. Annie would tell herself the story of that day—how they had to move every few minutes to keep up with the shade.

"We are still a family of two," Annie said in the dark while they waited for sleep.

"How else can I prepare for being a father?" Ben asked. "You get to prepare quite literally. You are growing her for us."

"I couldn't have done it without you," Annie joked, tugging at the elastic of his underwear. "And I can't still. Let's be in-love parents. Let's be parents who kiss all the time." Ben let her feather his neck with her lips, and he put his hands on her belly.

"Not in front of the baby," he said.

"You still love me?"

"Unequivocally."

Annie woke up early in the morning and wrote her dreams down, a thing she had never done before. She addressed them to the baby, like letters. *Dear Baby*, they went. Over on his side of the bed, Ben pretended to sleep, listening to her shuffling pen and thinking of writing letters to the uninspired mess in his abdomen. *Dear Guts, another day, another day.*

Ben went to work assembling a crib. He was sorry when he was done that the place his daughter would sleep came off a shelf with a hundred others like it. He was sorry that her view would be of bars.

"I want to build something myself for the baby," he said to Annie, as she sat with her feet on an upturned bucket in the yard. "What will she need?"

"She'll just need us at first. I don't think she'll be that into furniture."

"Annie. I need a job to do."

She smiled. "Why don't you build her a little table," she said. "I think little girls like to have little tea parties at little tables."

Ben liked the idea of a table where his daughter could put teacups if she wanted, or if she was another kind of kid—dirty socks or eagle feathers or stones. She could lay a cloth down and hide underneath. So he went to the beach and gathered driftwood. He imagined that it had come to him all the way from Asia, or floated up from a ship, sunk into the deep muck someplace. He hugged it to his chest, wet and salty.

THE TABLE WAS UNEVEN AND TIPPY, but Ben liked it and he called his wife in to see. Her face colored up. "That thing is practically *made* of splinters," she said. And then, leaning hopeless against the wall, "Do you have any *idea* how delicate her skin will be?"

Ben brushed his hand over the rough wood. He walked over to Annie, lifted her red sweater up and touched the side of her rib cage, recorded the texture of the skin in his mind. "Two thousand times more delicate than that," she told him. He pulled her sweater back down and nodded. He turned the table upside down and kicked the legs off one by one.

Ben threw the wood back into the ocean. He took his shirt off and threw it into the wind. He took his pants off and threw them too. It was cold out, windy spring, but he jumped into the bubbling waves and floated on his back with the dead table parts, hoping the ocean might continue to churn them all smooth until they were splinterless and appropriate for new skin. The gray sky fell toward them.

When Ben got out of the water and retrieved his clothing— his pants were spread out on the sand like they were trying to run away and his shirt stuck on a pile of seaweed—he noticed that, along with the tiny raised bumps of cold, the skin on his chest looked like a checkerboard or a grid.

He called Annie. He was shivering and his breaths were short. He explained the problem and they met in the hospital parking lot. He wore a winter coat and a pair of pajama pants he found in the trunk. She sat him on the hood of his old Datsun and he pulled his shirt up to reveal six perfect squares separated by half-inch-deep channels.

"Well," Annie said carefully, "there does not appear to be any redness or irritation." This was a practiced voice, a parenthood-ready voice. "It doesn't look broken," she added, optimistically.

"Nope, it doesn't look broken," he agreed. She swished her hand up and back, feeling the ridges.

THEY WAITED FOR TWO HOURS in the emergency room, where they read all the homemaking magazines.

"What did you eat?" Annie wanted to know.

"You think this is food related? You think this is from some bad chicken?" Ben snapped.

"It's from something." She opened her magazine and paged loudly.

"I'm sorry," he said.

She nodded. "You look like someone's ready to build a city on you. Property lines all set to go."

The nurse who finally called them in gave the battery of tests very slowly, glancing up at Ben's new feature every second or so, nervously. She fetched the doctor without bothering to make cheerful small talk. They could hear her on the other side of the curtain: "He has moats . . . He has squares."

The doctor had the nurse take a picture of him posing with the couple. In it, he made a serious face. A magazine-cover face. But he had no advice, only a tall pile of referrals. In the coming weeks, Ben and Annie scheduled appointments with the heart doctor, the dermatologist, the orthopedist, the cancer specialist, even the ear, nose and throat guy.

Annie woke up the following morning with her arm over her husband's side and she felt, extending out from his body, a warm, hollow box that seemed to be attached to Ben's chest. She screamed. She probably woke the baby, swimming in her pool of warm body fluid. She definitely woke her husband, who looked down at his chest and saw a section of it sticking out, a drawer. He sat up. He was barely awake, right out of a dream about an escape from a pack of dogs. He closed the skinless bone drawer with some difficulty, as it was quite stiff. In order to open it again, Ben needed his nails since it had no knob. None of these actions hurt. Ben looked up at his wife in her blue flannel nightgown. She was staring at him with wet eyes. "Look" was all he said.

BEN AND ANNIE packed up for a medical appointment in the afternoon, but it was one they already had: the ob-gyn, for Annie. While her feet were up in the stirrups, she asked the doctor if she had ever happened to see someone with a drawer coming out of his chest. The doctor did not answer, because she thought it was the beginning of a joke.

"Have you?" Annie asked again.

"No, why?" the doctor said, waiting for the punch line. But Annie just started to cry.

The waiting room was empty except for Ben, who had unbuttoned his shirt and sat there opening and closing his drawer. He had a small butter knife, taken from the dish rack this morning, to help him get it started until his fingers could fit inside and pull. He was smiling, running his fingers around the rim of his polished new cavern.

Ben reached over to the magazine table and picked up a pamphlet about STDs. He read through it and tore out a picture of a happy couple who were STD-free since they had been careful and followed the pamphlet's directions. In the picture, the man was wearing a bulky cable-knit sweater and was giving the girl a piggyback ride. Her brown hair streamed behind her and they were both laughing in a clean, sexually responsible way. Ben folded the picture up into a little square and put it in his drawer. He closed it most of the way, leaving enough space to get his fingertips in. He grinned and looked around the room. He opened the drawer a little and peeked in at the paper square. All that was visible in the dark of his own body were the man's white teeth.

Ben got up and gathered items. A yellow plastic magnet of the letter N from the kids' corner and a miniature lounge chair from the dollhouse. He tried a pen that said *Women's Center West* and had a picture of a uterus, but it was much too long so he put it back. He went into the bathroom and found, inside a closet, extra supplies. He took three Q-tips, one tongue depressor and a square of gauze. The tongue depressor had to be broken into thirds. He put them all in his drawer, happily. He sat down on the closed toilet seat and arranged his inventory alphabetically, starting with the picture because he decided to name the man Aaron. So it went: Aaron, chair, gauze, N, Q-tips, tongue depressor parts one, two and three.

Annie walked out into the waiting room with the doctor and looked around. No husband. She called. No answer. Figured he was probably in the bathroom. "Ben," she cooed. "Are you in there?" Ben buttoned his shirt, composed himself, opened the door.

"The doctor thought she might like to take a look at your chest," she said.

"I think it's fine. I think I just have a drawer now," he replied.

In a voice sculpted for use on a three-year-old, Annie pleaded gently, "I'm sure you're right. Would you let her just take a peek? Please?"

"I think it's fine," Ben repeated. "I think I just have a drawer now."

Her face became a square of irritation. "Pull up your shirt, Ben." She glared at him. And then sweeter: "We'll go have a coffee after this. At that place you like."

"I will pull up my shirt, Annie, but I think everything is fine. After this, I'm not showing my drawer to anybody else."

She breathed slowly and put her hand on her belly. "I'm not going to yell at you. Not in front of the baby."

The doctor rubbed her hands together, excited, when he began to unbutton.

"Oh, goodie," Ben mimicked.

OVER THE NEXT THREE DAYS, the one drawer was joined by five more. They were small, about two inches square, and pulled out halfway, seeming to have mechanisms that stopped them there. They were stiff and did not slip open when Ben bent over to pick up a fallen napkin or clean the shower drain, but were not watertight, so it was important that he dry each cavity out to keep it from getting dank and moldy inside. He used a washcloth followed by a Q-tip for this job, and the process extended his morning routine by six minutes.

Annie bought some apricot exfoliant, which she used on both her face and his chest, to polish it. The bone was bright white. Ben asked her to rub some of her cocoa butter ointment onto him because he found it soothing, though he had no actual feeling there anymore.

"This stuff is for mommies who don't want stretch marks," she told him.

"As soon as they start making a product for me, I'll switch."

He just liked the act of it, watching her long fingers rub the yellow goo in circles. She tried to pretend that she was not worried. At night she laid her ear up to his back, hearing the same heartbeat that she used to listen to in his chest. "I need you. We all three need you," she whispered. "Please don't stop beating."

In the evenings Annie still practiced Lamaze and did prenatal yoga with the women in her Mothers to Be group. She and Ben read through the shelves of books on child rearing, learned what to expect at each month of development post-birth. The cooing, the lifting of the head, the ability to wiggle on purpose—these were all things they could look forward to. Ben continued to attend birthing classes with her, but she caught him touching his own chest as often as the other dads touched their wives' round bellies. She'd elbow him. "Ben. Pay attention to *my* deformity now."

THOSE FIRST ITEMS from the doctor's office stayed. Ben came to think of Aaron, smiling from his pamphlet, as a friend and unfolded the paper occasionally to whisper hello. He didn't like the girlfriend as much and she never got a name. More things were stored in the drawers, too. He put a travel toothbrush and mini-paste in one and carried it around all day long, taking it out to use in the morning and before bed. His collection expanded to include loose change (useful, except that he didn't want to open himself up in public, so he ended up running out to the car anyway); a miniature jar of good mustard they'd bought on a trip to Germany; his father's pocket watch, which hadn't run in years; the ring he had bought his wife when they were first together: a round piece of amber set in silver. This he had stolen out of her jewelry box, but so far she didn't seem to miss it. He folded some paper towels up and lined the drawers with them so that the items inside did not roll around noisily.

When Annie and Ben went to the video store or the bank together, people placed their hands on Annie's stomach whether they knew her or not and asked the same set of questions: "When are you due? Do you know the sex? Any names picked out?" She answered politely while her husband stood by, ignored completely. Once, after an old lady had gotten her questions answered, Ben patted the protrusion and said, "Good sperm I've got. Good strong sperm, swam right up there and tunneled into that egg. Y chromosomes all over the place."

The next morning Ben went to the toy store. He picked out a soft doll for his daughter, one wearing a flowered dress with her string hair in two braids. At the register he said, "I'll also take one scoop of those tiny babies."

"You want the white ones or the black ones?" the woman asked.

"Well, maybe half a scoop of each."

The woman pushed her silver shovel into a basket and drew out a pile of bright pink bodies, and then into another basket, this time culling brown bodies. She poured them into a paper bag, tied it up with a twisty and handed it to him. Sitting in the car with the windows up, he took his shirt off and dropped babies into every drawer of his chest.

"Will you all need names?" he asked. "Each and every one?" He looked at the plastic bodies, who did not answer him. "Let's take it slow," Ben suggested. He decided to name one baby Archie after his first dog and placed Archie in Aaron's drawer, introducing them. To the rest he said, "Everyone can have a name who wants one. Just hang in while I think of some."

Even Annie adapted to the new feature. On their way to a party, she told him, "I'd rather not take a purse—could you carry my lipstick?"

Ben started to put the silver tube in his pants pocket, but she shook her head. "I'm not good enough to get inside?" she asked.

"I don't like to think of them as a convenience," he mumbled.

"Ben," she said, "I'm carrying our baby around for nine months."

He felt the weight of the tube in the drawer all evening, like a bullet lodged there. They chatted with separate islands of people about politics and giving birth and new restaurants. Ben watched his wife across the room, resting her hand on her stuck-out body, laughing. He watched her make her way to the dessert table and the drink table. She was lovely, drifting like a boat around the bay of this room. He would happily have blown into her sails, but they billowed already. When she wanted to touch up her lips though, she took Ben by the hand and slipped him into the bathroom. She unbuttoned his shirt.

"Kiss me now if you want to," she told him. Her finger was hooked over the lip of his open drawer.

He put his hands on her belly. "Look what we do to each other," he said.

She smiled, big and warm. "There turn out to be rewards, after all, to the empty spaces in our bodies."

"So do I always end up half-naked when you want to powder your nose?"

"See? It's not so bad to be my husband," she said. He put his lips against hers and held as long as she would let him, then sat on the closed toilet while she turned her lips, a wide expectant O, red. For the rest of the night, the tube was not a bullet but a hook, a hook with a long, shimmering line to Annie's mouth.

BEN'S ONLY REAL COMPLAINT was that the drawers were difficult to open. They limited his movements, too, but that ended up being a plus since his posture was suddenly perfect. But the opening and closing of the drawers was an issue. In the second month of the drawers, while Annie was out, Ben went to the hardware store and bought ten (in case some got lost) matching brass knobs, the smallest ones they carried. He threw in a chocolate bar and a bag of cotton candy with a picture of a clown on it, even though he knew that it was gross to buy cotton candy in a bag at the hardware store.

In the car on the way home, he took Aaron out and placed him on the passenger seat. "These knobs are going to be great," he explained. "We'll be able to use the drawers better now, open them and close them. They're attractive, too. These are nice-looking knobs." Aaron did not respond, but Ben was sure that he was behind the project one hundred percent.

Ben got his tools from the garage and made himself a cup of coffee and drank it while he ate the cotton candy. He laid the brass knobs out in a circle on the kitchen table in front of him. The truth was, he was nervous. He didn't know if the process was going to hurt. After his snack, he took some deep breaths and got out his drill. He took his shirt off. It was an awkward position, looking down at his chest with a power drill facing into him. He couldn't get a good angle on it, so he went to the mirror by the front door, where his wife always took final stock of her outfit and hair, one last check before she entered the world. He tried to line the bit up centered in one of the middle drawers, second row from the top. He went for it. It did not hurt in any measurable way, except he was aware that he was making a hole from the outside of his body to the inside. He winced as he worked, saying *ouch* out of habit and ritual, out of respect for his body, although he felt almost nothing. He screwed the knob on. It looked nice and shiny against the white bone.

Just as he was beginning the second one, Annie came blast-ing in the front door with no evidence of the groceries she had gone to get. She went straight for the bathroom, where she threw up. Ben tried to go in and help her but she cursed at him, and he waited quietly outside the slammed door.

"There is nothing you can do to help me!" she yelled. He tried the door and tentatively pushed it open when the handle twisted.

"Are you OK?" he asked with his eyebrows tight together. She was on the floor with her head on the closed toilet lid.

"Do I the fuck look like I'm OK?" she panted. And then right away: "I'm sorry. But also, fuck you."

"Can I get you something? I thought we were done with the

morning sickness." His voice was eggshell thin. She looked up at him for the first time. Her face fell flat. She looked desperate.

"I must have eaten something. What did you do to your chest? What is that *thing*?" He was happy for the change of subject and proud to show off his work.

"It's a knob! It's going to make it much easier to get them open and closed."

She thought about it and then shook her head decisively. "No. It won't work. It's going to look like you have a disease. Everyone will be able to see the balls."

He smiled. "You don't want everyone seeing my balls?" When she did not laugh, he considered her point. He kicked his left foot with his right foot. "Shit!" he yelled. "Why does it matter? Can't I have things sticking out? What are you so worried about?" He knew he was going to lose this one. She knew it too, so her response was measured.

"There's nothing we can do about the drawers. The drawers seem to be there for good. But we can control how obvious they are, and I'm sorry, Ben, but you can't have little balls sticking out. You're going to look like a robot with all sorts of buttons and toggles. No. Just, no." He looked like he had lost something important. She got off her knees slowly and moved closer to him, leaned against the sink. She put her hand on his face. "We'll figure something out. To make opening and closing easier."

Ben took the travel toothbrush out of his chest and prepared it for her, wetted and pasted. While she brushed, he sat on the edge of the sink and held his hands silently on the hidden baby.

"You are still the only miracle here," he whispered, though it was his wife he wanted to say it to.

BEN EMPTIED OUT the contents of his chest.

"Look what you've got in there." Annie smiled. "Look at all those babies. Diversity, I like that," she said, laughing.

Ben was embarrassed. "I bought them. I haven't named them all yet," he said.

"I'm sure you have time. What if we make little half-moon-shaped holes at the top of each drawer. Enough to put a fingertip in?" Annie asked.

Ben smiled. "I like that you called them half-moons."

"I'll need a lot of light. Go and gather lamps."

Ben sat on the dining room table, shirtless under the light of every lamp in the house placed around them on chairs, on the floor and the oval table. Everything in the room was made important by all that light: the dining table inherited from a grandmother though not well liked; the chairs, cheap and unmatching; the bulletin board with the collection of fetal images, those beans of babies in various stages of growth. The rest of the house was heavy, dark.

"How can this not hurt?" she asked. "I don't want to hurt you."

"I promise it won't. What if I read a story to you while you work?"

"No, I want you to watch me, to make sure I do it right."

Ben watched while Annie made the first cuts. He talked to her to keep her calm. "The baby has all of her toes already," he said, "teensy little nails even. She has her fingers and hands." His voice was deep compared with the high tink of the chipping bone. The pieces landed around Annie's feet like gathering snow.

Ben's neck became sore from watching his wife work. "The baby would like to know if she can have a pony," he said.

"Don't make me laugh," she said, smiling.

"The baby would like to know if she can stay over at her best friend's house and if she can have twenty dollars and if she can have a little brother or sister."

"Yes, on all counts," Annie said, and stood to kiss her husband, his chest wide open.

After she had made rough notches, she sanded them down. Even though Ben had no feeling in his chest, the vibration of the sandpaper went all the way though him, making his organs itch. They took breaks for this reason. Annie sat up on the table next to him, both of them kicking their feet like children on a tall bench. He pressed his hands on the baby. "What do you think about this strange family you'll belong to?" he asked her. She did not kick back.

"Have you ever tried to take one of the drawers out?" Annie asked carefully.

Ben shook his head no. "I do wonder what's in there. Same as you, I'd guess, and we don't propose to take you apart."

"No, we don't. Let's leave them in."

"I would rather. If it's all right with you."

When they were finished, Annie had made six holes in her husband's chest. He tested them out, one at a time, until all his drawers were open and his chest looked puffed out. "You look like a peacock," Annie said. "A proud peacock." Annie put Ben's collection back into his body. The piles of babies, the mustard, the tiny toothbrush, all of it. The two of them stayed in the dining room under all the lights and talked about baby names. She suggested mostly old-fashioned names like Annabelle and he suggested mostly names beginning with C, like Clarice.

Ben brushed Annie's hair with his fingers, which came away wrapped in a few golden strands. Annie pulled them off and laid them in a drawer already populated by brown and pink babies. The glisten of her hair disappeared into the dark of Ben's body.

"Can I keep those?" he asked.

"Those are yours," she said.

Annie stuck the tips of her fingers into Ben's new moons. Her arms hung like two sturdy bridges across the space between them.

Welcome to Your Life and Congratulations

I DO NOT FIND HOUDINI downstairs. Upstairs, my room smells like cat but has no cat in it. My bed is covered in the soft gray hairs. My parents' bed is also ashy-gray, the fur hovering and landing when I sweep my hand over it. I find my father and mother lying on the slanted roof outside their window, what they call the Veranda. They are squinting against the sun, shielding their faces. Their shirts are pulled up to make way for the darkening of skin. They glisten with sweat.

"Did you sell your lunch ticket?" my father wants to know.

"Fifty cents."

"What were they serving?"

"Sloppy Joes."

"You could have gotten a dollar."

"Have you seen Houdini?"

"You could have gotten seventy-five at least."

My mother says, "We aren't any fun up here. Why don't you go and play with Belbog, next door? He's come all the way from the continent of Europe."

"And can't you see we are tanning?" my father adds.

"I'm already nice to him on the bus," I tell my mother, and sit down on the roof's slanted face. I pull my shirt up too and reveal the stunning whiteness of my stomach.

"You can blame your father for that skin tone," my mother says. "Good luck getting any dates with any babes." She reaches out and takes my father's hand. She rubs each finger individually, gets her own into the crevices between them. Those canyons are completely explored.

Were the roof not covered in something like sandpaper, if it were slick—say, metal—we would all three slide to our probable deaths.

My mother lights a cigarette from the pack at her side and my father picks up his constant companions: a knife and stick. He whittles. My father is making another letter opener to be added to the drawers already filled with them. My mother's cigarette ashes get caught in the wind and circle all our heads.

"The best thing," my father says, "will be for you to save up for a trip to a country where they have beautiful women and you can marry one."

"What if I don't love any of the beautiful women when I get there?" I ask.

"By the time you got there, you'd see. The hard thing would be knowing which one you loved best. The world is just waiting for you, son," he tells me, looking up at the expansive heavens, shaking their rattles of sunlight down on us.

My mother says, "It doesn't have to wait—you're already here. Welcome to your life."

I see flat-faced Belbog, all the way from the continent of

Europe, walk out of his house and set up a card table and a chair on the sidewalk. He makes another trip and returns with three mugs and a pitcher of something red. He tapes a sign to his table, *Beverage For Sale.* He sits, his hands folded on his lap and his legs crossed, wearing a pair of large white women's sunglasses very long out of fashion.

Cars pass, not slowing for refreshment. They send wind Belbog's way, spread his hair out in the gusts. It is at this moment and from this incredible vantage point that I see Belbog's hair blowing, and in front of him I see Houdini cross the street toward home, looking like a ghost in the white light. And then I see a car, a red car, come around the corner and not even slow down for my cat, and not even stop after the noise that we all hear.

"Houdini?" I ask of the air. The cat is a pile in the street. Belbog jumps up and knocks the pitcher off the table, covers himself, soaks himself red. My parents jump inside through the window first, pushing me aside. And the long journey down from the roof begins. There are stairs I must go down. I must go through the living room and the dining room and the back hall and the front hall before I can emerge from the door, screaming the name of my cat. When I get down to the street, Belbog has the cat in his arms, legs loose and swinging, and says, "The car! The cat! The car!"

I try to hug Houdini away from him, to take him to my chest. But Belbog has him tight, so I hug both of them, Houdini pressed between the two of us, all our lungs pumping together.

"That cat's not going to make it," my father says. My mother has the portable phone and starts to dial, but he stops her. "That cat's not going to make it," he repeats.

"Call the vet! Call 9-1-1! Call the vet!" I yell.

"We shouldn't try?" my mother asks.

"It is hit!" Belbog says.

"He's old," my father says. "It would cost a fortune. It's better to let him die." The phone in my mother's hand is quiet and no numbers are pushed. I go for it but she holds it tight and I cannot get it free. "Let's take him inside," my father says, already walking, "where we can say goodbye properly."

"The cat will be dead from us?" Belbog asks, following behind the three of us until we reach the front door and I close it in his face. He stands there on the stoop, dripping onto the threshold of my home.

MY MOTHER PUTS a cookie sheet out on the kitchen table and I turn on the lamp above it, a spotlight. Houdini is matted with blood. He is not a gray cat anymore, he is a red cat.

"You have had him longer than you have had me," I say.

"We have had each other longer than either of you," my mother says, looking at my father. "The cat just showed up one day and I fed him."

"It would cost thousands of dollars, and even then," my father answers, "a new cat doesn't cost anything. The price of a ball-chopping, or not. If we don't chop the balls, we'd get kittens maybe. You'd like kittens, wouldn't you?"

"Honey," she scolds, "please." My mother holds the cat's two front paws in her own, she tips her head down to wipe her cheeks on her shoulder. "We would have kept putting food out for you. Milk. Leftovers."

"I have my savings," I offer.

"No amount of savings would be enough. He is going to go sooner or later. Sooner," my father says. The light swings just slightly, its halo shifting over the cat, who is less and less alive. I put my ear to his chest and listen.

"Hush-a-hush-a-hush-a," I whisper to him. When I come up, I can feel that my cheek is sticky wet. I rub the blood around. Rub it all over my face. This makes my mother cry harder. Flat-faced Belbog has his flat face pressed against the window, watching us. His snot drips out of his nose and down the glass.

"That's enough," my father says. "You are upsetting your mother. Goodbye, cat. Now is the time." He holds Houdini up above his head, and again the four legs swing and hang. "A freezer bag, honey," he says to my mother. Both of us follow him down the basement stairs. "Everybody needs to keep it together," he says. "If you try anything, I will kick you out of the ceremony."

"Can we at least sit?" my mother asks.

"Get comfortable," he tells her. We lower ourselves onto the bottom stair. She takes my head onto her chest. I can hear her heart going through its beats. My snot drips down out of my nose, it seeps into my mother's shirt, and I make no motion to stop it. My tears too drain from my eyes and soak through to her skin. Houdini's blood rubs from my cheek onto her chest. My face is stuck to her shirt is stuck to her skin. She says, "Hush-a-hush-a-hush-a," while I try to drench her, to soak her through, to drown her.

Houdini is still alive when he goes in the freezer. My father says he figures zipping the plastic bag plus the cold will do it. He does not want to hit the cat with a hard object. He does not own any guns, and a knife is out of the question. When he zips the bag, he says, "I'm sorry, cat. You are about to feel less air in your lungs. The cold will work to numb you."

My father sits on the floor with the freezer door open in the otherwise dark room. The only other things in there are some tubs of ground beef marinara sauce and the wool baby blanket my mother knit for me when I was born. She won a prize for it at the county fair and now it lives here to keep from getting eaten by moths. It is also zip-locked and its hair, like the cat's, is pressed against the plastic, smashed flat.

My father, his tools still upstairs, pretends to whittle—one index finger shaving the other index finger down. He looks like he is preparing to survive in the wilderness. The blue light from inside the freezer cleans him up and makes him shine.

"Should we say something?" my mother asks.

"Houdini was a good cat," my father tries.

"Houdini is in cat heaven, where there are rivers of milk and mountains of cheese," my mother adds, looking at me, watching for the happiness she hopes I feel.

"Houdini is in the freezer," I say, "and he is still alive."

My mother whispers to me, "We'll bury him in the morning. It will be a beautiful ceremony. When he is dead." She takes me by the arm, both of us crying, to the bathtub. I am too big to be washed this way and I say so.

"I want to be covered," I tell her.

"You will be, by water."

But it does not hide the few new hairs growing on my body. Even if I hunker down as low as I can, the water does nothing but magnify. Our falling tears cannot make this a sea deep enough for me to hide in.

"I wouldn't fit in the freezer," I say to her.

"You are not going anywhere," she says, and pours a bowl of the blood-pinked water onto my head. It rushes down heavy over my eyes.

EARLY IN THE MORNING when the light doesn't look like it is coming from anywhere in particular, my parents come to my door knocking. "Time to bury the cat," they say, like what they mean is "Happy birthday." In the kitchen there are scones, homemade. My mother must have been up for hours. They are browned and perfect, sitting in rows.

"Are those scones on Houdini's cookie sheet?" I ask.

"Houdini doesn't have his own cookie sheet," my father says. He has the shovel and he has a brown grocery bag. When I look at it, he answers a question I do not have.

"He's cold. I couldn't hold him."

"He's frozen," my mother reminds him.

THE EARTH IS FULL OF STONES. Every shovelful turns up more of them. They leave round crevices behind. When my father takes a break, resting his hands on the long wooden handle, I kneel down and put my fist into one of the stone's old homes. It feels warmed, like a just-left chair. Who knows how long that rock was there, sneaked down into the dirt, covered on all its ragged sides.

"The earth will digest him," my mother says. "He's free of his body now."

"That's enough hole touching," my father tells me. "Come on, son," he says, "let's get this show on the road." He returns to work. A pinecone comes up. A shoelace. Dirt, heavy and dark and wormy, comes up. When there is enough room for Houdini plus some, my father leans the shovel against the tree and turns the brown sack over. The cat is still in the plastic bag.

"We have to take him out of the bag," I say.

"It's OK. He's bloody," my mother says.

"For one thing, he won't disintegrate, for another thing, look at him." I go down onto my knees. I open the zip and try to dump him out, but he is stuck by his own blood to the walls. My mother and father stand over me, watching. I jam a stick in, try to loose the fur. The stick breaks. My parents do not suggest anything. I tear the bag off. Even when it goes, Houdini is still in the shape of it. His fur is still smoothed flat like something is pushing against it. Houdini cannot push back.

While dirt goes back in, I remove the worms one by one.

"You know they are part of the cycle," my mother says, and I do know, but it is too soon. For now I want to let my cat rest alone without being crawled upon, under the turned earth.

AFTER THE BURIAL I find Belbog asleep under my kitchen windowsill. He is not wet anymore but is still red. I tap him, wake him up, walk him back to his house.

"Have you been here all night?" I ask.

"Is he?" he asks.

"It's part of the cycle," I say. Belbog stands in the doorway and watches me. I right his overturned table and sit at it. Look at the street, at the spot where Houdini landed. The street is steaming with heat, already, even this early in the day.

"My name means White God, did you know?" Belbog asks.

"The continent of Europe must be very far away. Are there beautiful women there?"

"The most beautiful anywhere, my father tells me. I hope we will be friends. Perhaps this summer you can come and together we can sell beverages on the side of the road," Belbog says, and when he finally closes the door, I hear the lock slip, and then the other lock slip and a chain rattle itself into place.

WHEN I COME INSIDE, my parents are asleep on the couch, wrapped up in each other, the room full of morning light. I put a blanket over them. I take Houdini's cookie sheet upstairs. I look out the window at the elm, at the unsmooth patch of ground. I eat scone after scone, hoping that some of the cat was left on the tray. The sun is still a colored sun, not like later when the light will be so bright the particulars of it disappear. I go to sleep too, taking the cookie sheet under the covers. I can hear my father snoring through the floor. The spears of sunlight hit my back. They drill slowly into me, warming up even the deepest insides, and I fall asleep.

Again, my parents come knocking. "We have to hold a cremation," they say. "Are you ready? Put on your shorts." Out the window I see that the hole has been opened. Everything we worked to dig down has been dug up. My mother's hair is unbrushed. She is still wearing her nightgown and my father has only his underwear on.

"Dogs," he says.

"We can do a cremation here, at the house?" I ask.

"We build a fire," my father says.

"Obviously. And I put the whole cat in the fire?"

"There isn't a whole cat," my mother says.

"What is there?"

"Parts of a cat," they say together.

"Bones?" I ask.

"Mostly. And some fur. And some face."

The sun is now exactly overhead. The trees are sweating from the undersides of their leaves. The air does not move; it is a single object set in place. I am dripping by the time I leave my doorstep. Belbog is back out with his stand and a new pitcher. He is wearing all black. He waves. I do not wave back. Wood is taken from the shed and formed into a pyramid. I haul the three sun chairs together. My mother makes cucumber sandwiches. I walk across the street to Belbog's stand.

"I would like three glasses, please," I offer, and he pours.

He looks himself up and down. "We are mourning," he says. "I am wearing black."

"That's nice of you."

"No charge for the beverage," he says. "It is on my house. What are you doing now?"

"A cremation," I tell him. "Don't come over."

"If you need any more beverage, I will be here all day. I invite you to come and help me. We will split the profits fifty-fifty. Everything fair and even."

"Not today. I have plans."

I pass the cups out and put my drink-cooled hand on my mother's forehead. "Nice, isn't it?" I ask. She sighs and smiles under my palm. Even though her head heats me back up right away, I want to leave my hand there and let her burn it. Sear it if she wants.

The fire really gets going. It takes over the wood, sucking on it.

"Can I see the pieces?" I want to know. My father takes out another Ziploc bag full of bones and shreds. Both ears are there. There is a leg with a paw attached. A snout and nose.

"We can't put that right into the fire—we'll never be able to find it again," my mother says.

"Find it again?" my father asks.

"The whole point of a cremation is the ashes. We won't know which are Houdini's ashes and which are the wood's ashes. We have to sprinkle the ashes later, as part of the ceremony. To release Houdini into the place he loved best." My mother goes inside for a pan. Right away, the fur begins to sizzle away and the smell of it is everywhere. The smoke of the fire is turning my whole sky gray. It is closing in. I begin not to be able to see the street. The world is farther and farther away.

My mother goes inside and changes into a bikini.

"You look hot," my father tells her when she comes back outside. The fire is going and smoke is everywhere.

"I might as well get some color," she says, smiling. She lies back in her chair, puts a big hat over her eyes. She moves her toes to a beat that I cannot hear. Her fingers wrap around the ends of the armrests like they have been melted there.

"So," my father says, "your first burial and your first cremation, all in one day."

"I have never been alive without Houdini."

He gives Houdini's bone-pan a little shake. "We are doing the best thing." The bones have not turned to ash. They have browned a little and they rattle deeper when they hit the sides of the pan.

"The bones are still just bones," I say.

"We'll pound them if we have to," he answers.

My father closes his eyes and listens to the world around him. I listen too, trying to see what he hears. The fire spits and crackles. The bones spit and crackle. The fur has long since sizzled away, and the fleshy bits smell but make no more sound now that all the moisture has left them. There are birds everywhere, as usual. Cars pass in anticipated bursts. There is no danger that they will hit my cat. He is safe here now in his pan.

My mother starts up snoring and my father stands. "Sleeping beauty," he says, and goes to pee into the rose bushes at the edge of the house. I follow.

"She'd kill us if she saw us," he tells me, as our twin streams run in arcs and jump when they hit the green, green leaves. "I have a plan," my father tells me. "We are going to run in the sprinklers." His eyes are slippery and ready. "It's hot as shit out here. Let's cool off."

"We are in the middle of a cremation," I tell him.

"I am your father," he says. "I'm running the ceremony and

I know it's all right to take a break. Houdini doesn't need us right now. He will do fine without us. Your mother will keep track of him."

"My mother is asleep."

"This is your chance to celebrate summer with your father. No one else."

He turns the spigot on and water pours out in a fan. We strip down to our underwear and hold hands. We wait until the fan comes up over our heads, dropping pieces of itself onto our waiting hair. My father laughs in triumphant stabs. We are wet and wetter.

My mother sleeps her sleep and I do not go to her with a hand outstretched, do not help her open her eyes. This celebration is only for my father and me. She is missing everything and I let her.

"Now this time," he says, "I want us to high-five in the middle of the jump, right when the water hits us." When I leap, we smack our palms together. The water comes up and pummels the underside of my thighs. My crotch.

The water runs in streams all over the yard. Streams join with other streams and make themselves wide. They reach the fire. They surround it. They run inside and turn to steam. The wood is wet. The wood screams and goes soft. The fire turns to smoke, black and thick. The ashes of the wood are a gray mush. The bones of Houdini float in a gray soup. The smoke is blacker. The water is in my eyes and the smoke is in my lungs. We do not stop jumping. We do not stop lying down right in the sprinkler's path, where the water crashes down on our faces, shoots us full of holes.

. . .

I WAKE UP ON THE COUCH. The sun is heavy and orange through the kitchen window. I can hear my parents talking, laughing. I go to the doorway of the kitchen and watch them. My mother is still in her bikini and she is sitting on the counter. My father is wearing a T-shirt and no pants. He is leaning up against her, feeding her a piece of apple. I can practically feel how cold his skin is against hers. He pretends to put the apple in her nose. She laughs and turns away. He pretends to put it in her ear, and she laughs and wraps her head in her arms. He leans in and puts his mouth onto her mouth, and she uncovers. She does not turn away.

"Is it time to pound the bones?" I ask.

"Shit, kid," my father says.

"Can you go and collect some rocks?" My mother smiles. "Big ones?"

"Are you going to eat that apple or aren't you?" I ask her.

"Your job is to go and find a rock," she tells me, harder this time.

"We got wet in the sprinklers and you slept through it," I say. She laughs at me. "I know exactly what you are doing," I tell them and go outside. "You're trying to get rid of me. This family is getting smaller by the hour."

"This here," my mother says, motioning the small distance between the two of them, "is what made you. You don't even exist without this." I slam the front door as hard as I can. I collect one big rock. Belbog waves to me, then comes over. I hear the sound of my parents making their way up the stairs, then their voices through their open window.

"Business is slow!" he says. "Do you want to go climb something?"

"I'm in the middle of a ceremony," I say. He watches while I pull the bones out of the pan and put them on the doorstep, which is stained with something that could either be juice or blood. I hit them, bone by bone, smash by smash, with my big rock. They break into pieces. They get smaller. They get dusty. The dust gets into my eyes but I do not wipe it away. I keep pounding.

I pound until all the bones are gone, until they are a pile of gray.

"Do you want some refreshing drink?" Belbog asks me. "I could bring it here."

Belbog is sweating, dressed in black long-sleeves for our funeral even though he wasn't invited.

"All right," I tell him. "Yes. But I need to run inside for a few minutes first."

"Thank you," he says, and smiles.

"Will you please open the door for me?" I ask.

I gather the ash in my cupped palms, carry it carefully inside. Some of it catches on the air and drifts. I move as slowly as I can, keeping my hands perfectly still. I climb the stairs. I push open the door to my parents' bedroom with my foot and find them there, naked and stacked.

"You can't be in here," my mother says, grabbing for the covers. "We are doing something."

"I am doing something too!" I tell her, and I get up onto the bed, stand over them and make a crack in the cup of my hands. "Congratulations!" Ashes fall down over my father's back. "Good for you!" They fall over his head and coat the strands of hair. They fall onto his butt and onto the flat surface of the bed. They turn him gray. They stay in the air. The air is full of them, full of Houdini.

"Houdini is dead!" I say. "I love you and I hate you! Welcome to your life!" I throw the last of the smashed bones up in a cloud, a finale. I applaud.

Houdini surrounds us all. He is gritty on my parents' sweaty bodies. The sun makes his particles look like sparks. My mother and father are statues, gray and frozen, made out of muddy earth, as if they were the ones who had been buried alive. When they breathe in, I can see gulps of Houdini sucked into the holes of their mouths, coating even their pink gullets. All of us breathe the same ashy air—Houdini fills us up, binds us all together. When we breathe out, we send him in gusts, flying over everything that stabs, everything that reaches.

CONCEPTION

Catch and Release

AS BUCK AND HER SUPPLY BAG struck out through the side door, Mother Mom was lurking under the overhang waiting for her prey. She was a resourceful woman and always said she didn't see any reason not to make use of their bountiful wooded surroundings. Mother Mom had bird feeders set up every foot along the eaves of the house, probably two hundred or more of them, mostly homemade, and she hung out in the shadows with a large green net, catching whatever winged creature landed on whichever seed-filled box.

Her hands were webs of scratches and cuts from transferring the terrified creatures into the large metal cages also swinging from the eaves. She tapped her wrist—the sign that Buck should be home in time to help cook dinner—and they blew noiseless kisses at each other.

Beyond Mother Mom's bird terrain was Grandma Pete's shed, where she sat on an old office chair with her cane in one hand and a picture of her dead husband in his military regalia in the other.

"Good morning, Grandma Pete," Buck yelled.

"Good day, Lady Buck," she grumbled back. Buck joined Grandma Pete on the porch for the last inning of a baseball game on the radio. Baseball had come into their lives recently, after Grandma Pete found a picture of her dear husband in his handsome youth at the pitcher's mound. Listening to the game, Grandma Pete hit her cane against the floorboards at all the calls, good or bad, while Buck swung her pitching arm right along with the man on the mound.

"How's that look, Grandma Pete?"

"Sure," Grandma Pete answered, "looks like a pitch." When the game ended, they turned the radio off and listened to the outside world get its noises back. Grandma Pete started up telling the same four stories she always told about her husband: the day he left for the war, the day their daughter was born, the day he brought home a Christmas goose and four dozen roses even though it wasn't Christmas, and the day he died.

Buck didn't stay long. She wasn't in the mood for anything except tossing her ball around in practice for a major league baseball career in a future she hoped was extremely near in time and far in distance from here.

THERE WAS A THICKET in the woods with a soft grass floor and some low pine branches that made the whole place feel nestlike. There were blackberry bushes thorning their way over every other plant, and the smell of the dropped fruit rotting on the forest floor rose up warm and sweet. The thicket had a big clearing nearby that made a good place to toss the ball. Buck threw the ball one way and then ran over, found it and threw it back the other way. She had colonies of poison-oak blisters on her wrists from bad aim, so in order to improve, she set up targets where a pinecone was balanced on the stump of dead tree. She tried to hit the pinecone so it made a satisfying *thwap* and its scales detached and scattered like a firework.

When she got tired of going after the ball every time, she threw it up in the air and tried to get right beneath it, opening her hand so it had no place else to land. When she got hungry, she went into her supply bag for a pair of apples.

"You're eating two apples?" someone's voice said from out of the bushes. Buck stood up and looked.

"Who said that?" A man in an old gray military uniform came up to sitting. He had a black mustache full of dried mud. "You gonna kill me?" she asked.

"I won't kill anybody. You're eating two apples," he said again.

"One apple makes me hungry and the other makes me full," she answered.

"You can call me General," he said, and he put his hand out.

"Buck," she answered.

He told her, "It's been lovely to make your acquaintance. If you need anything at all, I'll be in this sunny spot making a list of what has been lost."

"You are absolutely certain that you won't kill me?" She thought about the promise teachers and parents always made her make about strangers. "Or kidnap me?"

"I swear."

Buck ate the rest of the first apple and the second one too, then wound up and threw the cores. They sailed into the trees and she didn't hear them land. "And it's gone!" she said in an announcer voice. The General sat with his eyes squinched up, and Buck chased herself across the tall grass while the bugs rubbed their wings together in one collective grind.

"So is your daddy into cowboys or something? Buck Rogers?" the General asked out of the quiet.

"Yes, sir. Was. But my mom was into First Ladies and they had it out." Buck's main plan in life was acting normal no matter what. She tried never to show fear, to always appear as if she was well acquainted with the situation at hand. "My real name is Mamie, after Mrs. Eisenhower, but no one calls me that."

The General nodded and stretched. "I suppose in this case they both won."

"I guess," Buck agreed, watching the General adjust his knee-high boots and his heavy coat, not at all suitable for this hot July day. "Have you figured out what's lost?" Buck asked.

"Oh, many things. My men. I'm going through their names, trying to remember all of them, first, middle and last."

"Where did they go?"

"Yanks got them." The General sighed. "Every time. Yanks." And this thought seemed to exhaust him in a way he hadn't expected. His arms flopped out on top of crossed legs. Buck sat as well and studied the two rows of brass buttons and the golden tassels on his costume. The jacket looked sort of like a dress, if a short one, and the pants ended at the knee, where the boots took over. There were a good many holes.

"So anyway . . ." Buck said, hoping this might get them talking. The man only nodded and looked up at the trees. They sat there in the heavy air for a few minutes before Buck got up and walked to the edge of the clearing, where she took her white ball out of her pocket and threw it as far as she could. Then she ran over, retrieved the ball out of the brush and threw it again. She jogged to meet it. The General sat watching while the ball traveled back and forth and Buck after it. After a particularly long throw, the General said, "Excellent throw."

Buck said, "Thanks. You think it's good enough for the majors?"

Then the General stood up and moved into position on the opposite side of the grassy space from the girl, who paused, confused for a moment, before realizing that she was being offered a second set of hands. Someone to catch and return.

"Could be, except you're a girl." Buck aimed and the General caught. Now it was only the ball that traveled back and forth and, outside of a few steps this way or that and the very rare dive, Buck stayed still.

"So what are you doing here?" Buck yelled.

"Throwing this ball!" the General yelled back.

"No! Here! What are you doing here?" Buck called.

"Being dead!" the General returned, along with the ball that Buck held on to while deciding whether to peel out and run for home or act natural. She was not a fast runner.

"Oh!" she tried out.

"I don't happen to be alive anymore!" the General explained.

"I see!" Buck yelled back, not really assured. They pitched and caught, pitched and caught, moving together slowly until they were in better talking distance. "Are you going to explain yourself?"

"When I was first killed," he explained, "I felt very dead. Blank. I could feel that my heart was still and that my spine was shut down. All around me there were other bodies, some in blue and some in gray, but all of them dead too. All of them blank and still. At one point, I stood up before I even realized it didn't make sense for me to try something like that, and, looking down at my bug-sucked body, I wanted to but could not throw up."

"Are you a ghost?" Buck asked.

"I'm a man who died. Whatever else that makes me, I don't know."

"All right, go on."

"I kicked and identified my men. Some of them had their arms out as if trying to fly, some faces down, noses smashed into the dirt, some faces up, eyes open, wind scavenging them. Oxygenating. Decomposing." The General looked at Buck's face and changed the subject. "I'm sorry. You know much about the game of baseball?" he asked.

"I know my favorite pitcher is Mordecai Peter Centennial Brown because he lost one and a half fingers to a corn shredder."

"I saw him play a game, as a matter of fact. Chicago, 1908, against the New York Giants. They couldn't hardly get a hit."

"You saw him pitch a baseball game in 1908?" Buck asked.

"I have had to keep myself busy. I tried going home to my wife when I was first dead. She couldn't see me. I sat at our kitchen table and watched her make a pot of soup. I watched her cut up a turnip and three potatoes. I watched her eat the soup alone while I was right next to her." The General stopped talking and let his head fall back. The trees were a frame for a flat circle of sky whose blue was sharp. "I left. I left before she even knew I was dead."

"But I can see you."

"Over time I learned how to toughen up my edges. By then, my Rosie was gone and there wasn't a home for me to be seen in," the General explained. "My wife was going to mourn me whether I was in her bed or not, and I couldn't stand to see it happen. I hoped Rosie and I would get to be dead together someday, and while I was waiting, I went for a walk. For a while it was a fresh sense of freedom every day. I didn't need to eat or sleep and I didn't get tired. I went to some ballparks and watched the game of baseball grow up. It was just coming around when I was alive. I found myself some nice spots by the ocean, which I had never seen before, and pretty much just looked out at it."

"You got bored and lonely," Buck said.

"I cannot tell you how bored I got. I have been dead for one hundred twenty-two years. My wife never showed up on the other side." They sat there in silence while Buck tried to imagine that length of time. She was already bored and lonely and she wasn't even thirteen yet. She stared into the woods, where the trees had their hands up to the sun, their tall noses in as much air as they could reach.

"You know what? No one in my family goes by their real name," Buck said, a cheerful offering.

"Is that a fact?" The General smiled, grateful.

"That is."

"If you tell me the story, I'll keep throwing this ball with you," he said.

"Better still, we can trade, one of mine for one of yours."

Buck began to tell him the story exactly as it had been told to her. A family history so well memorized she didn't pause once.

"POPS, THAT'S MY DAD, who was previously known as Dale, took to the road when he was sixteen on his motorcycle back in the Seventies, not because he was a hippie but because he had gotten wind of the whole free-love aspect and decided he was through hiding his naked magazines in three nested shoe boxes otherwise full of insect, rock and lost-tooth collections. His mother was a cleaner and a duster and he counted himself lucky that she hadn't stumbled on them yet. The motorcycle had been his own father's before his own father wasn't able to ride one anymore due to the loss of his legs in a war that was minor on the books.

"Pops had given himself that name the very minute he got out of his parents' driveway on his bike. He thought it would make him sound older and like more of an established lover.

"He never made it all the way to San Francisco, but he did talk a lot of long-haired girls out of their clothes, sometimes more than one at a time, and as far as he was concerned, that was all the success a man ever needed. He could conjure up every single one of those girls: name, date and length of leg, perfectly, without missing one. The only thing he added later was a mustache for himself, a nice thick one, when in fact at sixteen he had been little able to get three or four hairs to jut out at the same time from his soft upper lip."

"This is an awfully racy story for a kid," the General said.

"There is only one version of this story and I'm telling it to you."

"Is that the end?"

"That's the first part. Your turn," Buck said.

"I thought I might like to be a schoolteacher," the General started. He said he figured he liked children and he had some time but the whole thing fell through when he needed to produce a valid identity.

"I had no birth certificate or Social Security card or address. I went to the old folks' home instead, where people were much less concerned with safety. I befriended a few old people who needed someone to reach or water or sort for them, and what I got was company. It was good company too, because the old people had been around for a lot of the time I had. I pretended my knowledge of wars and economic highs and lows was from a healthy appetite for books. I kept them up late. We sat around Formica tables.

"Money came up all the time. What things were worth back then and how much you pay now. A hammer, a newspaper, a case of beer. We also talked about dying, which I had done but they hadn't yet. I couldn't warn them about it, though. They'd talk about being afraid to go or who had recently made the move. There was always somebody. I tried to be helpful, saying things like 'There's much more ahead,' but really this thought made me very sad. I would have liked to tell them that they were almost finished."

Buck spat on the ball and threw it high and hard, but the General was fast and caught it.

"The minute they removed the bodies," the General remembered, "the manager came and took the plants. She kept the good ones for herself. Her office was a jungle of dead people's greenery. They wound their leaves around her desk legs and up and out the window. The walls were hardly even visible through the foliage. The rest of the plants, the ones she didn't want, she lined up outside the dining room. Those were usually the first sign the old people got that someone among them was gone. They guessed by the plant who it might be, tried to remember each other's apartments: who had a ficus in the corner, who a plot of sweet peas in that window box painted with dancing elephants."

The General paused.

"We only have what's growing outside," Buck said. "Nothing alive in the house but us girls." She dove for a ground ball.

"Turns out you've got hands like magnets," the General said, at which Buck grinned. It's possible to pitch without a catcher but you can't do the opposite, so Buck hadn't known she was playing the wrong position all along. Here she was jumping and sliding, getting the ball every time.

"I'm pretty good," she admitted.

"You have a definite talent," he said as he threw a hard one her way. "I expect you'll be able to get yourself a scholarship if you work at it. I believe it's your turn."

"OK. Mother Mom was born an Annie, but I started in calling her Mother the way Annie called Grandma Pete. But Annie said she'd rather be Mom since she felt old the other way, though instead of swapping out, I just tagged on, and from then on the woman had two names that meant the same thing.

"Annie had become a mom because she wasn't shy about calling Pops 'Pops' and she wasn't shy about what he wanted from her, which kept him coming around a few nights a week. Though they never intended to make a baby out of the situation, pretty soon he took the saddlebags off his bike and unpacked them into the drawer that had been cleared out, all except for a little hand-sewn sachet of pine needles.

"Now, Grandma Pete used to be Grandma Mae until Grandfather Pete died several years back, and she took it as her personal crusade to make him as remembered as a man could be. That was also when she moved into the fixed-up shed behind our house and when she started in loving the game of baseball. She found an old shot of Grandfather when he was in the service playing a game, him at the center of the triangle and a lot of cottonwoods as a backdrop. Handsomest she ever thought he looked. She wanted to make some more copies of that photograph. Come to think of it, she wanted to make some more copies of a lot of photographs. With the help of Mother Mom and me, she covered every inch of wall in her shed-house with pictures of Grandfather Pete. We blew them up and shrank them down for variety. On a long Saturday, the three of us climbed on chairs, stools and ladders to nail up stacks of those photographs so that, in the end, his face looked in from every direction.

"The only places where he wasn't staring out were the flat surfaces where Grandma kept her collections of trinkets—bears, moose and fairies. 'A woman has to have a place for herself,' she always said, dusting them off with her fingertips.

"When the walls were covered, Grandma walked down to the county clerk's office and had her name officially changed.·

The last time she'd been in that room was the day she and her husband-to-be went to get their marriage license. That first time she took his last name, and this time she took his first. She put her old white hand on the counter and asked to be officially renamed in the eyes of God and everyone. The boy filled out the paperwork and got the right signature and sent the old lady out into the afternoon sun with her husband's name."

The General encouraged Buck with a steady smile.

"That's it," she said. "Since then it's just been us and the birds."

"What about your story?"

"My story?"

"Buck's story."

Buck scrunched her nose. "It's the same as my family's story. As of today I guess I can add that I met you and discovered I can catch even better than I can throw. Your turn."

"This next part requires acting."

"Sure," Buck replied.

The General didn't know the name of his killer, so Buck stayed nameless. She was told how to spring out from behind a short hill, in this case imagined, and how to weave between bodies. Buck's important line was "This is your end," to which the General yelled, "But it isn't the end of the war!" Before they got there, though, they each fought several other men. The routines were carefully explained to Buck, the General standing behind, his arms wrapped around her, all four of their hands grasping a long branch while they shuffled forward and back, slicing the air. They practiced the scene a dozen times, with Buck ending by hovering over the General every time, her fist around an imaginary knife. "This is your end!" she seethed. She got very good at delivering that final line, her teeth clenched, her face hot.

The light was low by this time, and a fleet of swallows circled overhead catching evening bugs. "I think we're ready for the real one," the General said. He handed Buck a short, sharp stick to tuck into her sock. Buck and the General took their places in the clearing and battled imaginary soldiers separately, the sound of their branch-swords making wind as they cut back and forth. They breathed hard and mumbled at their opponents before turning on each other. They followed the steps of their dance perfectly, each putting the other in jeopardy, losing control and trying again. They cursed each other and dove for the ground after dropped weapons. Finally, in the last moments, Buck pulled her stick from her sock and held it over the General's heart as he lay on the ground staring up, his eyes reflecting the purple of the sunset.

"This is your end," Buck grumbled, and drove the stick into the General's chest. She felt more resistance than she had expected. The General yelled back at her, "But it isn't the end of the war!" and he coughed and spit and made choking sounds that were absolutely realistic.

"Hey," she said. "Hey. You're fine, right?"

"The story of Buck is just getting going," he whispered. He held his chest with one hand and with the other he blew her a kiss. "Catch," he whispered.

Buck could see real pain in his eyes until he relaxed onto his back and his arms fell away and he was still. Suddenly Buck wasn't sure about anything. She looked at the man with the stick in his chest and then at her own hands and the pinecones and at the darkening forest, and Buck began to run.

She tore through the woods, kicking up leaves and hitting her shins against low branches. The forest was noisy with evening feeding traffic not limited to the swallows, who continued to swirl overhead. Rustle occurred in the underbrush all around, and bugs occupied the middle region between ground and sky. Buck's own breathing and stamping and crushing of whatever was on the earth in front of her scared up squirrels, who darted off in every direction.

She got the quilt-squares of lighted windows in her sights. As she approached, she saw her mother lying on her stomach on a flattened plastic sun chair, a cage full of songbirds hanging above her. Buck did not slow her run across the lawn and came to a halt all at once when she could crawl under the chair, her back flat against the sun-warmed stone and her face exactly below her mother's, whose nose and cheeks were smashed against the plastic. Buck put her hands on the underside of the chair, on her mother's stomach. The blue weave had absorbed the heat of the body on top. Buck could feel her own heat rising up, the sweat fighting to evaporate against air that was already full of moisture. Her heart had not slowed yet. A drip of spit hung down toward Buck. It was a jewel. Buck took it on her finger and ate it.

Mother Mom woke up suddenly, surprised.

"It's me," Buck said, pressing. "I'm home now."

"Hello, Buck," Mother Mom said. She did not seem surprised to be acting as her daughter's protective canopy. "You all right?"

Buck nodded and pressed. Mother Mom scooted up so that her face came over the top of the chair.

"Catch anything?" Buck asked just for the sake of niceness, because she could see and hear that her mother had.

"I caught you," Mother Mom said, and she smiled and reached her arms around and took hold of the small hands below.

THE STORY OF Buck's own name was the only one she had wrong, but it wasn't Buck who was lying. Indeed she had Mamie on her birth certificate, after the president's wife. But Pops, who had been very angry about the existence of any baby because it meant the end of his roving, ranging, free-love life, and who also had no interest in cowboys whatsoever, had come storming into the hospital room where Annie and the new bald girl were lying. She nursed her and petted her soft head. When he saw the baby, he pulled his wallet out of his front pocket where he always kept it, for safety. "Here!" he yelled, throwing a one-dollar bill at the bed. "This is my contribution! Call that baby Buck, 'cause that's all he's worth!"

"It's a girl, Pops," Annie said, her eyes sharp.

"Even worse," he growled as he marched out to his bike, revving it outside the tiny hospital so that it made the baby's head vibrate ever so slightly on her mother's chest.

The dollar bill hadn't floated more than three inches from the place Pops had stood, and it stayed there for exactly one hour while Pops sat on the side of the road throwing stones at the carcass of a smashed cat. He hadn't expected the baby to look so vulnerable and for Annie to look so beautiful holding it. Truth be told, he hadn't even gotten around to thinking it might be a real actual living thing, since he'd been busy all nine months stewing about the damper it would put on his excursions. Not that there were really so many excursions anymore. The fact was that Pops had been staying with Annie for months anyway and had tried only once to pull another girl's skirt up, and up it went, but he, sadly, could not get himself to do the same, so he dropped the girl off at home, having apologized and bought her an ice-cream cone.

But he didn't go back. He rode on, left his things in the drawer, left the baby with milk passing into her open mouth while her mother dozed. The doctor came and after checking some boxes on a chart, he noticed and took the dollar bill on the floor, stuffed it into his breast pocket, where it traveled all day until it was taken out in the cafeteria in exchange for a bag of unsalted peanuts.

Annie called Buck "Buck" as if it were an apology and a tribute to Pops, as if it were the least she could do. But she never told her daughter the truth of her name. In the family legend, Pops had been a fan of cowboys and had gone off to find a ranch for his own lovely daughter to raise horses on, her hair shining in the dry, red sunset.

GRANDMA PETE was in the kitchen playing solitaire with the picture of Grandpa Pete propped on the chair next to her. "Hi, Petes," Buck managed. Her body was buzzing like it was full of a new substance: not blood anymore but something rattling and dry.

"All right, line up," Mother Mom commanded, and handed out tools. She gave Buck her mallet and Grandma Pete her cleaver, got herself a wastebasket and put a large cutting board in front of each of them. In the center of the table, she put down a platter and a bowl of marinade. Theirs was a well-practiced assembly line.

Buck reached her hand into the cage, where it was scratched and pecked until she caught a bird, and then held it on her cutting board and knocked it on the head with the mallet. There was a delicate *crack* like a blown eggshell. She passed it on to Grandma Pete, who took its head off and gutted it, her hands slick with red and the bowl in front of her a squirm of guts. Mother Mom plucked it naked, while her own blood-sticky fingers became covered in feathers.

"Do you ever see Grandfather Pete?" Buck asked her grandmother.

"What's not to see, dear?"

Mother Mom started humming against the noise of wings constantly crashing against the cage bars, striking them so they sang like guitar strings.

As they passed their work around, the women's hands met for split seconds, the skin at varying levels of elasticity, varying levels of heat. Their fingers were slippery and eager to touch one another. Slowly the room quieted down until there were no more screeching birds in the cage and the plate in the center of the table was a hill of slumped pink bodies soaking in butter and homemade wine.

. . .

BEFORE THE LONG RITUAL of sucking tiny morsels of meat off needle-thin bones began, and while the smells of cooking rose out of the oven, the most delicate underfeathers, having escaped the broom, were airborne again and again with even the smallest human movements.

The women went outside, where Mother Mom and Grandma Pete cheered for Buck, who threw the beaked heads, pitch by pitch by pitch, into the usual place.

"That must have been ninety miles an hour, that one," Mother Mom hollered, and Grandma Pete said better than that. The woods offered up the many-legged creatures from deep within the bramblebush to catch everything Buck threw. Life crawled over other life, devoured it, opened itself up to whatever it had been given. The whole world squirmed with hunger and desire, in the thick and thin places, in the trees and in the clearings.

Saver

MABEL LADY FINCH lived with her dad in a one-bedroom apartment (the living room was hers) in a complex with a pool and weight room that neither of them had ever used. She could have afforded to move out, but she didn't want to leave her dad alone. He wasn't really completely alone—he had a girlfriend who, Mabel expected, would hang around for the usual month of romancing, then she'd split just like the others. It was like Charlie, which was what Mabel called him, had been given the first volume of a two-volume set on love. At this particular moment, he was still in the first course of a relationship with a woman named June August.

"They figured, no reason you can't have two months in your name. No law against that!" she explained, while Mabel did their spaghetti dishes. She tossed her stringy blond hair. Charlie put his hand over her knee in a cup, carefully, like she was a firefly he did not want to damage. Mabel left the kitchen and sat down on her pullout that was not pulled out and read some of her City College psychology textbook, which surprisingly had a picture of a skier on the cover.

Mabel looked at the picture of Lady holding her when she was just born, the picture her father had asked her to keep to herself since it made him too sad to see his lady love holding, tenderly, the cause of her death in her arms. June and Charlie, in his bedroom, made very little sound. So little that Mabel knew exactly what they were doing.

Later, in the late dark with her one little lamp on and the room dressed as a sleeping place, Mabel heard her father knock on the wall dividing them.

"Baby?" he loud-whispered. She knocked back, tap, tippety tap.

"Hi," she said.

"She's no good, is she? June August?"

"She's fine," Mabel returned.

"Should I tell you about your mother?" The two of them did not read books together; Charlie did not sing. What he did, had always done, was tell Mabel stories about Lady.

"You know the one about when she adopted the puppy without consulting with me?"

"I know that one."

"What about when we tried to go camping and ended up stranded in the snow with nothing but a butane stove to keep warm?"

"I want to know the one about when she learned she was going to die."

"What about the one where the old woman mistook her for Audrey Hepburn?"

"That's not the one I want to hear."

"She didn't want to leave us."

"Do you think about her when you're with June August?"

"I think about her when I'm with everyone."

Mabel waited for more. There was just quiet and house noises though, the refrigerator keeping cold, the very low buzz of the lightbulb that you really had to want to hear.

THE DENTIST in whose office Booker Cyranowski was a new hygienist was so nice and his teeth were so perfectly white there was no way not to trust him. He even bought Booker a ham-and-cheese croissant on this, his first day, which was delicious.

They talked about the business. The dentist gave Booker some tips on how to keep nervous people from biting. He told a few dentist jokes that would otherwise probably not have been funny, but in this case Booker laughed so hard a little bit of ham went flying out of his mouth and landed right on the dentist's collar. The dentist just brushed it off with a napkin, patted Booker, whose eyes were huge and terrified, on the hand and said, "Son, I'd rather have that on my shirt than stuck in your teeth." The way he said it made Booker want to curl up in the crook of the dentist's armpit and fall asleep. He thought of drifting off to the sound of the dentist flossing carefully in the dark. The squeak of the string on his teeth.

In the elevator, the dentist used a rubber gum pick and Booker stood still with his hands clasped behind his back. He wished he had some instrument to prove how orally hygienic he was.

Out of the corner of his eye, Booker noticed that there was something drawn on the velvety wall of the elevator. He turned to look and saw a picture of a penis and the word *Shit*. He did not want the good dentist to see something obscene—especially since it didn't even make sense—on his nice elevator, so Booker quickly rubbed his hand over it back and forth to erase it. The dentist looked at him quizzically. "I wanted to check and see if the wall was as soft as it looked," Booker explained quickly. The dentist squinted his eyes and continued picking his gums for a moment. Then he turned to his right and rubbed his hand over the wall.

"That *is* soft!" he exclaimed. "I've never touched it before. All these years and I've never touched it before!" He said it like he had just discovered that there was a bright blue lake right behind his house, hidden in the trees, full of trout, with a pier and a nice little red rowboat. He put his hand on Booker's shoulder and smiled like he was staring out at this most beautiful vista. Like there were cranes in the sky above the turquoise water, and snowy peaks, and naked ladies lying on a cluster of warm boulders.

"Do you have one of these? A Gum Explorer?" the dentist asked.

"No, sir. But I'd like to get one," Booker said. "I'd like to get one right away."

MABEL HAD ONLY BEEN WORKING Canned Foods since mid-morning. She used to be in Produce, which she preferred. She would rather eat it and she would rather stock it.

It was during her break that things changed. "You look sexy when you eat that carrot," Mr. Joseph T. Bowers III, Manager, said while they sat in folding chairs in the back of the supermarket amongst boxes of discontinueds and damageds. He leaned down and kissed her forehead with his warm, horrible lips.

Mabel kneed him in the groin and watched him curl up on the floor like a bug.

She got moved to Aisle Nine and told to keep her mouth shut.

Now she had to go through the things that had been long unsold and "refresh" them. The unpopular and dusty hearts of palm and cocktail franks. There were a lot more cans in that aisle than she would have guessed a few days ago, back when her primary concerns were weeding out soft limes and fluffing the Swiss chard.

"Does this suit you?" Mr. Joseph T. Bowers asked, looking at her with greasy eyes.

"Get out of my aisle," she said.

In the afternoon, while she was doing the garbanzo beans, a woman came into Aisle Nine and started pulling cans off shelves at an unusual rate. She was wearing tight zebra-print pants and a black blazer with most of her breasts sticking out. She noticed Mabel looking at her and smiled a big, glowingly white smile. She put her hand out, offering a shake. "Jessie Mc-Fleece," she said, "Can Opener Gourmet Cookbooks." Before Mabel could even respond, Jessie McFleece went into what was obviously a well-rehearsed PR speech. "Truth is, I'm lazy," she began. "I'm always cooking up a new way to save time." She winked and said, "Pun intended! I'm going to try a lasagna to-night." Mabel looked into the cart. Nothing but cans: mushroom soup, carrot spears, bright green peas, and stewed tomatoes. Tuna, meatballs, spinach.

"Yum," Mabel said.

"You betcha. My kids L-O-V-E it. Husband doesn't mind it so much either. We are just a regular old American dream." They both looked at her chest.

"You know what? I need a better reason to live," Mabel said. "If anyone asks, tell them I quit."

In the parking lot, Mabel came upon a fellow employee. She untied her green apron with the words *Saver! The name says it all!* embroidered across the front. She stepped on it. "You can step on it too, Booker," Mabel said to the boy. He was humming and shifting back and forth on his feet as if he was warming up for a waltz. "You look like you're in a good mood."

He leaned in close and whispered, "Actually, I started a new job today. As a dental assistant! I'm just here to get my last check."

"Congratulations. We both have something to celebrate, because I just quit. Good luck at the new job." She paused for a second. "I hope you like teeth." He smiled and offered her a stick of gum. She put it in her mouth and saved it up in her cheek, feeling the sting of its spiciness against that soft flesh. Booker tore the plastic cover off a rubber toothpick and began to run it along his gum line. Mabel tried to smile. "I can see you're committed," she said.

"Look, I live across the street and I have a friendly cockatoo. Come over and eat dinner with us. I'm a harmless dental assistant."

"Have I just ruined my life?" Mabel asked. "My father is going to be furious."

"Are you allergic to anything?"

"Not that I know of."

"Then come on."

BOOKER CYRANOWSKI had worked at the Saver for years, since the day he graduated from high school and took his old Cadillac, which was the nicest color green he'd ever seen on a piece of metal, down the very familiar farm road, out the highway and on up the coast.

"Bye, rabbits," he yelled out the window to the rabbits. "Bye, tree," he yelled to the scrubby little pine in the middle of the sage and matted grass. "Bye, birds!" That one he screamed at the top of his skinny little lungs so they would hear it. He turned up the radio and swooped his hand in the wind.

Behind him he knew his seven brothers and sisters and his mother and father still stood out front with their hands on their hips. They'd go back to the strawberry field later, they'd pick since it was the end of picking season. Booker's Polish father, Bruno, and Mexican mother, Estrella, would take turns reading to the whole team, as they were called, stories of revolutionaries for whom the children had been named. Cesar, Rosa, Martin, Che, Coretta, Zapata, Booker, and the youngest, Andrej, named for Bruno's grandfather who had, as family legend went, carried all four of his children on his back all during the First World War.

Booker imagined them together in the little living room,

over a pot of beans and kale. He was the oldest and the first to leave. His parents were proud to see him head out, to fight the good fight. They were sorry, too, that he wouldn't be working the earth with them. But in his mind he saw the symmetry: his family grew food to sell that was chewed by the teeth of the people, the very same teeth he would someday be cleaning. As he drove, he thought of all those teeth, healthy in their nests of pink gums.

Booker bought himself a toaster at the big department store, and a cockatoo at the small pet shop. He had always wanted a bird, and without his family he figured he would get lonely. In the pet store, he put his finger through the cage bars and asked her in a quiet and high-pitched voice if she liked to be read to. She was pink and he named her Sue, after no one in particular.

IN HIS APARTMENT, Mabel found that Booker had books. Most of them were about birds, lots about the Civil Rights Movement and the Mexican Revolution, and a few about the state of Arizona, where he confessed he'd never been. Booker pressed Play on his answering machine and a man's voice came out.

"Dear Booker," it said. Booker talked over it to tell Mabel that it was his dad.

"He always leaves messages like he's writing a letter," he explained. "He comes from another time and place."

The message went on. "Dear Booker, it's your dad and your mom and everyone, and we know it was your first day of work at your new job there, and we are very proud of you for going out and doing it, like you always wanted to. The team loves you. Yours, Dad."

Mabel was holding a book in her hand, *The Sonoran Desert*.

"I'm into the outdoors and I think saguaro cactuses are amazing," Booker said, opening up to a dog-eared page. Mabel read the highlighted sentence, "The outer pulp of the saguaro can expand like an accordion, increasing the diameter of the stem and, in this way, can increase its weight by up to a ton."

"Wow." Mabel tried to care about the cactus, because it was clear how much Booker did. But the real excitement was Sue, whom he took from her cage and brought over to Mabel on his index finger.

"It's OK, you can touch. She's Sue the Cockatoo." Sue the Cockatoo checked Mabel out and seemed mostly to approve. Mabel stuck her finger out and Sue beaked it. Mabel made bird noises and Sue made no noises. Then Sue made bird noises and Mabel made bird noises and felt good, like they had connected. Booker put Sue down on the table and she walked awkwardly around.

Mabel watched while Booker stuffed two Cornish game hens with two whole hot dogs each, nested together and sticking out the back of the birds. He hummed and rubbed dried oregano and butter on the pinky-white skin. The birds went in the oven. Then Booker shucked corn, a few of the silky strands falling on the floor. Mabel collected them and braided them together. Booker opened the dishwasher, which was empty, and put the two ears of corn inside, in the place the silverware should go. "My mom's special recipe," he told Mabel.

"I see." Mabel thought for a second. "And they cook in there?" She paused again, though he was nodding.

"They steam."

On the couch, they drank sparkling cider out of coffee mugs. His had a picture of a rainbow and said *3rd Graders Are Number One*, and hers had cats on it whose bodies spelled the word *LOVE*. They polished off a bag of Fritos. Booker told Mabel all about Sue the Cockatoo. He got her when she was a baby, *just a hatchling*, he kept saying. "She likes peanuts in the shell best. That's her chocolate pudding."

"I like chocolate pudding, but what I really like is tapioca," Mabel said, a little tired of talking about the bird. For a while they discussed desserts. Neither one liked cake: too cakey. But both loved pie. "You can come over to my house sometime and I'll bake you a cherry pie and we can eat it outside with our fingers," Mabel offered. "But I live with my dad. Shit. Can I actually use your phone?"

She dialed her home number. "I'm sorry," she said, twirling the cord around her finger until her skin turned purple. "I miss you too. Order some pizza or some Chinese food. We can have it again for breakfast. Don't forget about street sweeping tomorrow. I know, Dad, I'm sorry. I love you."

The dishwasher-steamed corn was covered in butter and tasted good and sort of clean. They laughed hard when Mabel went to cut a piece of meat and accidentally shot a hot dog out of her tiny chicken's tiny chicken-hole and onto Booker's plate. He gave it back to her. "Your hot dog, madam," he said.

"Much obliged."

They lay down on the floor to let the food settle.

"So why did you quit?" Booker asked.

"That motherfucker Mr. Joseph T. Bowers tried to kiss me in the break room this morning."

"Will you sue?"

"Nah. I kneed him in the balls. And he's already fat and lonely."

"Here," Booker said, patting his chest. "I'm sorry that happened."

Mabel looked at him. "You're a nice guy, right?"

"I'm a harmless dental assistant."

She listened to his body make alive-noises. She thought about what it would be like if those noises were louder, if all the time when people were walking around buying turnips and drinking cappuccinos they could hear the juices in their guts making high-pitched squeals and low burbles. If they all had to speak up to compete with their own intestines.

"Where did you get your name?" Mabel asked.

"I'm named after Booker T. Washington. My dad's really into civil rights."

"Didn't he invent peanut butter?"

"No, that's George Washington Carver."

"Oh. Apparently it's been a long time since fourth grade." Booker's stomach made a long, howling screech. "Did you hear that?" Mabel asked.

"Hear what?"

"It's very busy in here. Amazing." She poked his belly. "You know, I didn't used to like my dentist, but now I have a pretty good one. I like the free toothbrush," Mabel said, and then before she could stop herself, "I have a retainer."

"My mom has false teeth that she soaks in an ashtray at night," Booker offered, laughing.

"Wow."

"Where'd you get your name?" he asked.

"It was my grandma's name. My middle name is Lady, which was my mother's name. She died due to complications after childbirth. I guess you could say I killed her." Mabel's hands got slippery and she tried to ignore the picture of her father sitting in the living room of their grubby apartment this morning cleaning his boots with the end of a chopstick. "I have an idea," Mabel said. "Why don't you check and see if I have any cavities?" She lay on her back and opened her mouth as wide as she could.

Booker looked carefully inside, tooth by tooth.

"You have a mercury filling in number twenty-two. You might think about getting a porcelain one someday . . . I'd need tools to really tell, of course, but your teeth look good to me. You have nice, strong molars," he told her, and he came so close that she could smell his spit, and she kissed him, one fast-and-over kiss on the mouth. "We could know each other really well," he blurted out.

And just like that, Mabel saw a crack form on the surface of her life. An opening. She did not know if it was deep or shallow, or where it led, but she did know something that did not exist before had begun to exist now. "Do you know who you are, without your family? Who only you are?" she asked, without meaning to. Mabel did not know why she'd asked the question. She felt blood rush to her cheeks and wished she could have said something normal. Complimented something manly about

Booker, or simply given him the coy, sexy glance she knew she was supposed to have practiced. But Booker did not pull away from her, or look at her like she was a crazy person, or even sigh. He squinted at the ceiling, and thought, and then Booker whispered, "Pretend we are two huge saguaro cactuses, side by side in the rocky ground."

Mabel wanted to know the answer even if it belonged to another question. "OK. I'm pretending," Mabel agreed.

"Our arms are wrapped around each other's necks. It is warm out and we are growing bright pink flowers. Our spines prick into one another's four-hundred-year-old skin and the water inside us seeps out in little beads. We could survive without rain for months. You can't believe how many stars there are above us, just millions. Everything around us is alive and busy, but all we have to do is stand still. The small birds that make homes in our bodies have left us alone in the dark."

Snow Remote

POST-THANKSGIVING, this was Leonard Senior's territory: pacing up and down the 100 block of Sapphire Avenue, his trigger thumb all the time ready. He wore a red sweater, the same red sweater every evening, tucked into a pair of slacks. A reindeer with a flashing red nose was pinned over his heart. He was lit up in red, green and blue by his homemade light display; the animatronic and the flashing. The whole block was lit up, in fact. The neighbors across the street had a separate set of heavy drapes made for these months. Their measly store-bought light-icicles hung limp and drooling toward the ground. Their palm tree was bare and brown, not wrapped in Christmas glory but standing with its one big foot in the earth, sulking.

Leonard Senior waited for a chance to snow.

LEONARD SENIOR and his teenage twins ate dinner together, but tonight, like most of the cool nights of December, it was a brief affair. Leonard Senior boiled the water and heated up the cheese mix while Leonard Junior poured the salad into a bowl. Then Junior watched the macaroni while Kerralyn set the table. "Don't make much for me," she said, "I have a date."

"Tonight? A school night? Wouldn't you rather go out on a weekend?" her father asked, his disciplinary sword undrawn.

"No, sir," she answered. "This very night is when I'm going out. It's a dog-eat-dog world out there, buddy. I'm not the kind of girl to get the Friday date, but I rate for midweek."

He said, "But I think you are perfect."

Kerralyn told her father she appreciated that and she would do her best to work her way up to weekends. "Baby steps," she told him. "I'll try for Thursdays this year. Maybe Mom has some advice." She smirked, looking at the urn on the mantel.

Her brother did not say that her date was ugly and stupid. He did not say that if he was lucky he would get a Monday date, Monday *afternoon* probably, everyone home in time for their sorry family dinner. He sat down at the table, where they each dipped their fork into the large metal bowl in the center of the table and ate directly off it. They had never stopped setting the table with plates, but they hadn't used them in years. Every night, Kerralyn set them out, and then when they finished eating, she piled them up and replaced them in the cabinet.

"Well, we're coming right up to the big day," Leonard Senior said.

"You got your stocking all ready, Dad?" Kerralyn teased. "You got your list for Santy?"

"Your mother would be so disappointed in us," Leonard Senior said, looking at the urn surrounded by a pine sprig and two candles in silver holders.

"She probably *is* disappointed in us," Leonard Junior corrected. "Right this minute."

ON WEEKNIGHTS, people did not pass by often. Leonard Senior paced, his thumb always poised, the whole block and beyond lit up by his very own house. Santa rode his sleigh across the rooftop, an abbreviated two reindeer pulling it along. There was a dancing gift box that went up and down and a snowman who waved. Inside his one store-bought item—a giant inflatable snow globe a good seven feet tall—Mary, Joseph and baby Jesus were always out in the cold, always covered in a dusting of white flakes. Mary and Joseph sat up and the powder gathered on their heads, making little white cones out of them, but Jesus, lying flat on his holy back, had the stuff all over his face. The undersides of his body were newborn pink, but his smile and eyes were deep in a layer of plastic flakes.

A couple in shorts and sweatshirts rounded the corner. Leonard Senior cleared his throat and made several circles with his thumb to prepare it.

"You folks hear the weather report today?" he called out. The couple looked at him, confused. "They called for snow!" he yelled. "Right here in Southern California!" The man released his arm from the hook of his girlfriend's elbow, a move that seemed to signal his readiness to defend them both against this information. Just as the woman began to say, "Where did you hear that?" a jet of artificial precipitation shot out of Leonard's house and fell down on all of them, melting on their sleeves. For one short and glorious moment, a few feet of sky was filled with snow, and Leonard Senior squinted so hard his eyes were nearly closed. He imagined that when he turned his head down, the ground would be covered and he would have to go inside and change out of his sandals and into a pair of real winter boots.

"What do you know!" Leonard Senior laughed. "They were right!" The couple smiled generously and touched the dampened speckles on their arms. "Wow," they said, clearly without meaning it, "isn't that something."

Upstairs, Kerralyn and Junior watched from chairs by the window, their feet in tubs of warm sudsy water, a rainbow of nail polish bottles lined up on the sill. "Those poor motherfuckers are never going anywhere now," Kerralyn said, scuffing the dead and useless skin off her heel. Junior filed down the nails on his left hand so short that the hidden edge was revealed, a tender arc of nerves.

"I'm getting in the bath. You should time Dad and see how long he keeps those people," Kerralyn said.

"What about your toenails?"

"Reggie is picking me up at eight. No time."

"Reggie is a shit ass," Junior said.

LEONARD JUNIOR, alone in the window with his feet pruned and pale, ignored the perfect view down at his father's bald head and looked instead at the phone next to him. He took Bess's number out of his pocket. He compared her script to the even shapes of the numbers on the phone. He mapped out the movements he would make if he were to dial.

Bess was a lady who worked at the candle store at the mall. Things with Bess had gotten to the next level, flirting-wise. She was older and so free of all the high school associations. Junior wanted to take her to every place he had ever been. He put the paper down and picked up the receiver, listened to the question mark of the dial tone.

"Oh, hi, Leonard."

They talked about Bess's roommates, two women each with one baby, and about her shitty electric bill and her shitty gas bill and her shitty landlord. Junior tried to be sympathetic.

"They should give you a raise," he said.

"Hell yeah, they should."

"Plus I think you are very skilled. I mean, like, what's the difference between the Fall Spice Apple, the Apple Pie and the Cozy Winter Apple?"

"That's easy. The Fall Spice has nutmeg and clove, and the Pie has some kind of crust smell, I'm not sure how they do that, and the Cozy Winter pretty much just has a different label from the Fall Spice but the same smell, so I'd say you should choose based on your décor. Like if your room is more red or orange toned, I'd go with the Spice, whereas if you've got more white or sparkle themes, you're better off with the Cozy Winter." Junior splashed his feet in the pan of water and beamed. Here it was Wednesday, and if he pulled at its edges, he could almost consider this a long-distance date, their two voices running together like water.

"See that?" he praised her. "You have a real gift."

"For candle smell at least," she admitted, modestly.

They talked about people who annoyed them and things

they wished they could afford. Then Bess said, "All right, Leonard. Tell me about my boobies. What are they like?"

"Oh," Junior said. "Well," Junior said. "Your boobies," he started, "are like Fall Spice apples."

"Hmm." There was disappointment in her voice.

"They are like round and juicy Fall Spice apples," Junior tried.

"Juicy, huh? Do you want to suck on them?"

"Sure, I'd like to suck on them. I bet they'd be delicious."

"I bet they would too."

Junior did not actually bet they would be delicious. He bet that they would taste like skin, though this did not stop him from wanting to try them out.

"Pretend that you are," Bess said, and Junior looked for something on his own body that resembled a breast. He settled on his left knee and sucked it and licked it right into the phone, transmitting slurping noises into her ear.

"You are one hot papa, Leonard," Bess said through some moaning.

"And you are one hot mama," Junior added, but this turned out to be a bad thing to say, because once it was out there, the word *mama*, he felt his own mother, dead and ghostly, descend down on him from wherever she normally was. He felt her perch on his shoulders and put her ear to the phone, listening for every exact dirty word that came out of his mouth. She probably did not like Bess or think that she was the kind of girl Junior ought to call up in the first place, and when Bess said, "I'm going to take off my shirt now and you should too," Junior felt his mother's breath on his forehead, and he hung up the phone.

"Kerralyn!" Junior yelled, walking to the closed bathroom door. "Kerralyn!" He heard drops of water fall off a lifted leg back into the tub.

"What the hell do you want?" she asked from inside.

"Do you think Mom can see us all the time?"

"How the fuck should I know?!"

"But do you *think* so?"

"Do you mean like, can Mom see my naked-ass body right now from heaven or something?"

"Yeah, do you think she can?"

"Maybe. But I would rather not think about that. It's not my damn fault if she looks."

Junior considered this. "Can I come in?" He heard the metal slide of the shower curtain and then he opened the door and sat down on the closed toilet and said to his sister, hidden behind the undersea-themed plastic, "OK, then, how would you describe a boob?"

"One boob?"

"Boobs, however many."

Kerralyn waited a second, then said, "Like a round globe of milk."

Junior nodded. "What's holding the milk in?"

"Who cares? You asked me to describe a boob and I did."

"What's the nipple then?"

"A fucking huge chocolate chip. I don't know."

"Fine. What else. Tell me about your stomach," Junior said. "What's it like?"

"It's like a feast," Kerralyn replied, "of smooth whipped cream."

Leonard Senior slammed the front door behind him. "It's a verifiable blizzard out there!" he yelled up the stairs. "It's three days to Christmas and the snow won't stop coming down!" His laughter rose up to them, through the floorboards and the carpet, where Junior was clothed and Kerralyn was not, their bodies, whatever they were like, hidden from all mortal eyes.

When Leonard Senior was younger, not yet a Senior, just a Leonard, not even young anymore really, after what could not have been described as a prime was over, he met a woman. She was younger than he but also not young. He met her at an all-night diner, where he bought her a piece of strawberry pie and a plate of onion rings.

He said: "You look lonely like how I feel."

She said: "I have no idea how you feel."

But she let him sit and watch her eat. Leonard revealed details of his loneliness—the proximity of television to bed, the white space of the refrigerator, the phone sitting quietly by the front door, and the light on the answering machine holding steady, never blinking. The woman did not look at him when he talked but moved the heavy strawberries around on her plate, mixed them with the whipped cream to make pink slop, which she placed carefully on her tongue with the tip of her first finger.

"You know where I want to go?" she asked, and without waiting for an answer, "Jamaica." She began to sway as if to slow reggae music. "I think I would like to live there for the rest of my life."

"What would you do for money?" he wanted to know.

"Fuck it, whatever. Sell shell necklaces. I'd be good at

that—I like to make things." Leonard pictured her sitting on a white beach with coconut palms reaching high above her head and water playing at her toes. He said, "That sounds good."

"I hear you don't even need a passport to go there. Just a bikini and some damn flip-flops."

"And some sunscreen," he added. "And I bet they have bad mosquitoes."

"Some fantasy you've got."

Leonard Senior took the woman home with him. She got into his car and after that she got into his bed. He turned the television on and they made love to *The Golden Girls*. Love was not precisely what they made, but they did make something. A thing that later, Leonard Senior, with his eyes red and his hand squeezing her hand, the two of them sitting back in that diner, this time with only coffees for a meeting she had called, first begged and then paid her to keep. "I will give you one thousand dollars, I will give you one thousand two hundred dollars, I will give you fifteen hundred dollars." She sat there, eyes down, looking into her cup while the money in her invisible bank account went up and up.

"Will you give me fifteen hundred dollars, plus all medical expenses, plus a ticket to Jamaica?" she finally said.

"Yes, yes, I will do that."

"OK. But I want nothing to do with this little sucker," she said, holding thumb and forefinger in the measurement of one inch. Leonard did not know if this signified the size of the baby or the size of her love for it. He got the idea though, and he sat back with his feet crossed at the ankle and smiled up at the stained ceiling. He ordered up two pieces of strawberry pie when the waitress came.

He did not know yet that there would be two babies instead of one. That the boy would be named for him, the girl named for a woman who did not exist. He did not know yet the lie he would make up to explain the absence of a mother. He did not know yet about the trip he would make to the crematorium, where he would manage to purchase an urn, empty, and fill it with the ashes from his own fireplace, or how he would place it on the mantel of that same fireplace with a story about a beautiful wedding on the beach and another about a car accident.

KERRALYN SAT ON THE CURB waiting for Reggie Lazzarino, Leonard Senior stood at his post and Leonard Junior poured a tall glass of milk and sat down by the telephone upstairs. He watched his sister and his father not talk. He watched his father point at the light display and his sister not look where he pointed. Then he watched a car pull up and Kerralyn get into it and close the door. He watched his father watch her do this. He watched his father send them off in a single flurry of snow, hardly enough to celebrate by.

Junior thought about Bess in her apartment with her room-mates watching television. In his picture they were eating baked potatoes, a thing that seemed adult and womanish to him. The potatoes would have a little butter and some broccoli florets and a single slice of white, never orange, cheese melted on top. Junior was nearly certain of this. He picked up and held the body-warmed phone in his hand until it began its noisy reminder that no one was on the other end.

In the street his father got lucky. A large group gathered around him. The snow machine was in the crook of the roof, just outside where Junior sat. When the button was pushed, his entire view was snowed out for a few seconds and he couldn't see the reactions of the group until the storm had fallen below his line of sight.

Leonard Senior waved up at his son, a strong salute. The room was quiet. The phone did not ring and later it did not ring some more. Junior gave himself a second pedicure and manicure and finished his milk. He plucked the hairs that bridged the distance between his eyebrows with his sister's tweezers like she had shown him. In a sudden moment of bravery, he picked up the phone again.

Bess said, "What type of shit was that?"

"I want to tell you about your boobies and your stomach."

"I'm on the other line, Leonard. It's going to be a long call."

He started to say, "I'd like to take you to every place I've ever been," but somewhere in the middle, she was gone, replaced by the phone's over and over cry that its job was over, it had endured his wet breath and stupid words and wanted to be replaced now in its blue cradle.

Junior wrapped his arms around his own chest like they were someone else's arms. He rubbed his hands on his back like they were someone else's hands on his back. He imagined that his fingers were tipped with painted nails and that they were slender and long and so soft he would have to comment on it to the owner. "Your hands are so soft," he would have to say, because it would be true, and Junior believed in telling the truth. In this room though, there was only him, his upper body twisted up into a neat knot.

Junior went downstairs and tried to watch television, explaining each segment of the show during the commercial break to his mother, as though she could hear him but not the TV, as though his voice alone could travel the distance. "She's a nice girl, Mom," he said to the urn. "What would you want me to say, if you were a girl? Would you want me to tell you I loved you? That I would love you until everything in the world was completely used up?" His mother did not answer him from above or from inside his head or from anywhere.

IN THE CAR, Reggie Lazzarino had everything laid out perfect. When he picked Kerralyn up at her house, there was a single red rose on the passenger seat.

He said, "Wow, you look like a dream," and then later, "I can't believe how beautiful you are." When they ate burritos, he looked into her eyes the entire time and asked her about her wishes. Reggie said, "Kerralyn, what do you wish for?"

Kerralyn said, "I don't know. I wish for money, I guess." Reggie nodded soulfully, like she had said something profound. "What else is worth wishing for?" she asked him.

"You're a really smart girl," he answered.

They shared a cookie and he drove to the edge of the cliff, where the ocean looked like a terrible hole. He said, "Kerralyn, if you want to really know the truth, then you'll have to know that I want to kiss your lips."

She said, "You don't have to sweety-sweet me anymore, Reggie. We have now come to the part of the evening where the bullshit stops."

He said, "You're a really smart girl," and they smashed their mouths together, he smashing more than she, she actually having to pull away slowly because it felt like her face might break open, like he might unhinge her jaw and leave her with her chin hanging free, the dark passage into her throat permanently visible.

Once they had de-shirted and Reggie had his big hands on her breasts, Kerralyn asked him, "What are my boobs like?"

"Tits," he answered, stupid.

"I mean what would you compare them to?"

"Why compare them to anything else? Tits are the best thing they could be."

"Then what's my stomach like?" she asked him, pulling her head away.

"The stomach of a pretty girl," he said, touching it.

"A metaphor. Say, 'Your stomach is like soft cream,' or something."

"It's like a platter of buttery dinner rolls," he said, squeezing.

After this, Kerralyn did not ask any questions. When Reggie put his hands beyond her dinner rolls, she sat there in the passenger seat, unmoved. He unbuttoned and unzipped and breathed onto her so close that her neck had rounds of moisture on it. "This is nice," Reggie breathed. "You are a very smart girl," he breathed. "Your legs are like . . ." but Kerralyn stopped him.

"Just be quiet," she said. "Don't talk to me anymore." So

Reggie stopped talking but did not stop maneuvering the vehicle of his hand over her, plowing roads through the wilderness.

When he finally crawled over, released the seat all the way back and wriggled his hips into place, Kerralyn was so quiet and still, her only presence in the car outside of the heft of her physical form was her heat mixing with his, making a bubble around them both. The windows were opaque with it. They were white with it. They were heavy and beginning to drip.

"I want you to call me Reginald," Reggie said, "like my father." Kerralyn did not call Reggie anything. "I mean right now," he corrected her, "I want you to call me Reginald like my father right now." Kerralyn still did not call Reggie anything, so presently he started to do it for her. At first it sounded like he was prompting her, like a baby, as if when she heard it again she would repeat. "Reginald, Reginald, Reginald," he said. But soon he was not listening for her echo anymore; he had gotten used to her silence and filled the small space with his own voice and his own name. "Reginald, Reginald, Reginald, Reginald," he chanted, his butt hitting up against the dashboard. *Will this get me to Thursdays?* she wondered. *And what must you have to do to be a Saturday girl?*

Kerralyn closed her eyes and watched the bright shapes behind her eyelids and listened to Reggie breathe and repeat his name like this was the last minute of his life and he wanted the universe to remember him, he wanted to prove that he was here, that in a world of Andrews and Marcuses and Tyrones, he was a Reginald in a line of great Reginalds and this moment was no different. This moment was a flag he was staking in the ground so that it might wave in all manner of future winds.

. . .

FROM THE UPSTAIRS WINDOW, Junior watched his sister exit the date car. Her hair was lit by the Christmas display, green and then red, glowing. He could not hear the sound of her footsteps as she walked toward her father, who pressed his button and snowed on her.

Kerralyn slammed the front door and Junior heard her yell, "I'm sorry, Mother!"

Their father paced while the last flakes landed and died on the sidewalk.

Junior watched his father walk out to the middle of the street and put his head back. The sky looked back at him, empty and snowless; the heavens were unpunctuated. Junior slid the window up and began to toss things down, one at a time, precipitation for his thirsty father. Pencils, pennies—which smelled like a fresh cut—the cotton balls Kerralyn used to remove her nail polish. Senior did not notice, lost in the night, in the street. Junior carried the sloshing pedicure pan to the sill and tossed the water out as hard and fast as he could. Still, his father saw nothing of the small storm.

Junior wondered what kind of weather it would take—what kind of hurricane he and his sister would have to make—for his father to finally come inside, gather his children in his arms and secure the windows. Leonard Junior was furious then that they lived in California, where the winds and clouds never conspired to close the roads, take out the phone lines and the electricity—Rudolph relieved of his constant red-and-green leap forward and back, and baby Jesus? For the first time in his holy little life, the bubble around him would tear open in a gust, and he would feel the weight of real water on his cheeks. The family would be confined to the house, where the cupboards would burst with supplies, and the warm, uneven light of candles would remake the room, soften everyone's faces. They would sit silently holding hot cups and listening to the rain whip at the door but never manage to blow it open.

LOVE

The Ages

WHEN THE GIRL AND THE BOY moved in together, they had sex in the bed and everyone could probably hear it. Houses were pretty close together and there were a lot of open windows. Neighbors must have talked about such a carefree afternoon of loving all week, hushed whispery talk while taking the trash out and untangling the wind chimes. While hanging the *Happy Thanksgiving, Pilgrim!* flag out front. But what could the girl and the boy do? Their young bodies were young and bodies and they weren't going to stop the rolling around or pushing together on account of proximity to other, older bodies. So they kept it up and they even walked around afterward naked, only closing the most obvious curtain. Whatever the air was doing that day, whatever water was or wasn't falling, the sun and the crooked light—they wanted it inside.

Hands went all over the girl and boy's raggedy hills. It didn't feel like just two bodies in a bed. The girl saw everything in the history of the world in their love—dinosaurs munching the most delicious dinosaur grass, and the smell of cooking chicken and a mountain covered in something mossy and desperately soft and the wind was there, and the sun hit down on everyone's various cheeks and the two of them, the girl and the boy, stood palm to palm in the middle of all of it.

EVERY EVENING IN THE NEW TOWN, the girl and the boy went walking. It was a big-window kind of place due to the ocean view. Lives were on display. Knickknacks and upholstery and kitchenware. Vases of calla lilies and a quiet mess of bills piled on a dark wood desk. The things were owned, as far as the girl and the boy could tell, by a lot of old people with very regular schedules. The white-haired woman in a button-down shirt sat alone at the glass-top dining table with a plate of potatoes and green beans, mashed and steamed. A hunched and tiny man in his big living room, modern art on the walls, watching reruns. The nurse a couple feet away, one eye on his breathing, the other on her foreign newspaper. Mondays and everyone had the football on, burying their socked feet under a pillow to keep warm.

Once they discovered them, the girl and the boy didn't want to miss the happenings outside. They felt as if their future was being presented to them: *Here you are in sixty years*, the world said. *Here you are in twenty*. The girl and boy put their jackets on and went out to see. They saw the old men and old women enjoying glasses of red wine and, on weekends, pieces of frosting-cake. The men and women power walked. The time was over to stroll, those youthful days of enjoying the view ahead. They wore matching jumpsuits and carried foam-covered comfort weights and listened to FM radios. Their bluey-gray hair was smashed down under headbands.

The men and women brought with them little dogs who snuffed along in their kneelessness, trying to keep up. Who shat on the sidewalk. The girl and boy were surprised to see that men and women often left the little dogs' shit where it lay. Right in the middle of that good ocean view. It got stepped in. It smeared brown over the sidewalk. The old people had to stop at the next bench and break a stick off one of the potted plants to clean their glistening white sneakers. Some were so disgusted they went straight home and threw the shoes away. Some did not mind so much and continued power walking the shit right off the shoe. They had no time to waste, Their lives were disappearing out from under them by the second. Unstoppable, those ones.

There were people in the town who still worked, whose houses were empty except for a woman who came to vacuum the floor and a man who came to trim the vines. There were dogs in these houses who were not brought out for walks and stood jealous on the furnished porches with nothing to sniff but their own deposit on the Adirondack or the terra-cotta. The girl and boy figured the little dogs craved something new, something Doberman or basset hound, but it wasn't in the cards most of the time. Such was the life of a dog with an unretired owner. The girl and the boy decided the owners probably had the stock market numbers memorized by the time the coffeepot began to burble. Their ties had a closet to themselves. Audible love was past, but power walking still waited ahead in a future that the unretired hoped would also include polished golf clubs and visits to only the most comfortable of foreign nations.

On a day when the smell of apple pie rose out of all the kitchens and all the people were dressed in fall browns and oranges, the girl and the boy came to a house they had passed dozens of times. Now a wheelchair sat empty on the deck with a sign attached: *Mae Peterson 1922–2006 Funeral on 12/27 at 2:00 p.m., St. John the Worker.*

"I'm sorry, Mae, whoever you were," the boy said.

The girl found a rock nearby and placed it on the chair.

"What are you doing?" he asked.

"I think it's traditional. I wonder if she was satisfied with how things turned out."

"She died right here," the boy said, looking into the flat, unlived-in living room.

They stood there until it got dark, watching the empty wheelchair. And the stream of little dogs continued, and the stream of improved lifestyles continued, and as evening poured out, lamps were switched on and people cut their chicken into perfect little bites and the warm pie flowed smoothly down their throats.

FOR CHRISTMAS the power-walking town was covered in white lights and mechanical singing Santa Clauses, from every rooftop, window box and doorframe. Men and women, especially those with children as visitors, were all set for unwrapping and ham. The girl and the boy, sitting at their little table with a single candle flame jumping between them, said to each other, "Merry

Christmas." They tried to kiss a little. They tried to think about the next year rolling up onto their feet like sea foam, soft and welcoming.

"Will we know what to do when we are thirty? When we are forty-two?" the girl asked. The boy shrugged. "Will there be a day when you decide to get the newspaper delivered and then another when your cholesterol numbers become part of our regular lives?" He shrugged again. "I don't know anything about wrinkle cream or about being a mother."

"I don't want to know until I have to," he said. He took her smooth hand. "This year we will try some new vegetables. We'll listen to some new music. That's all." The girl closed her eyes, where the darkness was filled with unanswerable questions.

"But you love me, right?" she asked.

"That is exactly what I do," he said.

They decided to go out and see the special moments taking place all over on this Christmas Day. The families sat at the big table and forked pieces of meat and mashed potatoes. They ate the oven-cooked things and the pan-fried things and the ones that went pan first, oven second. They bit into the pumpkin pie and placed fingerfuls of whipped cream on their tongues, while the girl and boy stood on the sidewalk and looked on. No one invited them in and no one smiled at them. The girl and boy did not ask for those things and they weren't sorry not to have them. Watching was enough, witnessing all that life. They joked about the dishes they did not have to do, the fights they did not have to have with frustrating uncles.

Candles did their dances across the length of the white lace while the diners updated one another on the outlines of their lives. From the sidewalk, the girl narrated for the women and the boy narrated for the men. "She's reminding her father to settle the matter of the upstairs carpet," the girl said.

"And he wants to know if she's gone to the dentist," the boy added.

"Those two over there don't usually get along. They fight about each other's spending habits," she said.

"Now they are laughing at the story the aunt just told about a minor car accident." Steam rose from the dishes a lot at first, a little, and then barely at all, except through a crack between lid and body of the soup pot. People picked their forks up less and less often and everyone started to lean down, heavy, toward the floor.

It was dark and cold out. The light from the strands over the windows was crisp.

"Should we go home?" the boy asked.

"Not yet," she said. "What would we miss?"

A lot of the houses were dark now, the toys flung down and the flannel pajamas worn for the very first, and perhaps last, time.

"Are they satisfied with the birthday party for their Lord?" the boy asked. "Do you think they had a good time?"

"Yes. But they're tired. It took a lot out of them. Now they're trying to get ready for the New Year. They have to plan for everything that will happen."

"The reduction of their thighs, for example," the boy said.

"Don't joke," she said, "they have a lot to worry about."

The old man in the biggest house, with his couch that stretched the full length of the living room, facing out at the sidewalk, was an unmoving lump there. His small, wrinkled body covered maybe a quarter of the brown leather. Under his blue plaid blanket, he looked like a fish about to be devoured by his enormous house.

"Do you think he's OK?" the girl asked.

"Sure he is," said the boy.

"What about Mae Peterson?" the girl asked.

"Just because she died doesn't mean the whole place is going to drop."

"One person dying doesn't stop another," she said. "Let's stay here and keep watch." She almost thought she would feel better if she got to see someone die. Like skipping ahead to the end of the book. After that, all the particular events in the middle don't matter as much: they go to the same place. The moon was making its regular attempts at light. The boy's and girl's hands were white from it.

The girl was sure the old man was dead now, sure that soon his nurse would return and put her ear up to those drooping lips and gasp because there was no air going in or coming out, and she'd call 911 and pretty soon ambulances and fire trucks would be there making their whirling calls, and all the neighbors would come out to watch, standing around the girl and boy, in their bathrobes and glasses. Their hair mussed from sleep, their slippers soaking up the dew on the ground. The paramedics would wheel the old man out on a stretcher, and everyone would whisper what a nice man he was and a few people would look covetously at his house and wonder if they could afford to buy it now or if it would just get passed down anyway.

The moon traveled from the top of the sky to a few inches

from the bottom. It began to pinken and the dogs and their walkers started to come out. The blue-haired women in their shiny black suits came out of big doors with small dogs and started to power walk into the day. They adjusted their radios and their waistbands and headed out. They had big Christmas dinners to burn off now, step step step step. Their old-lady hips went back and forth. They waved to each other. "Jean," said one woman to another, loud, over the sound of her oldies, "you look as skinny as a rail."

The other woman waved her hand dismissively and said, "Oh, Anne, you're too kind." They both smiled and power walked on, not even looking down at the girl and boy cross-legged in their path.

"We could go home now, to our own house," the boy said, but the girl shook her head.

"Not yet," she told him.

When the morning light was at full volume, the men and women got into their cars and went to the mall to return all the unwanteds in exchange for amazing bargains.

The boy asked, "Aren't you hungry?"

"No one else is paying attention," the girl told him. "We have to be the ones to see what happens."

And then, while everyone else in town was preparing lunch, the man on the couch simply got up. He sat first, then stood.

"Is he a ghost?" the girl asked.

"He's a man," said the boy. The man let the plaid blanket fall next to him. He stretched, reaching far above his head. He was tall and his skin was like a cloak draped over his arms.

"What is he doing?" the girl asked.

"Maybe he needs to go to the bathroom. Maybe he wants a cup of coffee. Maybe someone will come to visit him today."

The girl began to cry. "How does it end?" she asked.

The boy went to the door and rang the bell. "How are you?" he asked when the man answered.

"I'm excellent," said the old man. "But I'm having my breakfast. Can I help you with something?"

"Happy New Year," the boy told him, "was all we wanted to say." He motioned to the girl out on the sidewalk, and the old man waved to her, smiling. The boy waved too, his young hand and the man's old hand like flags from neighboring countries. They smiled at either end of life, and the girl could see real, definite happiness in their faces.

The girl and boy wrapped themselves together in bed that afternoon, the curtains drawn against the sun.

"My gift to you is this," the boy said, kissing her neck. A lineup of porcelain bears, given to the girl by her mother over a series of birthdays, looked on. The bears played dumb. Didn't even shift to chat with one another. Just watched with their big sloppy eyes while the boy and girl tangled themselves up and breathed into each other's mouths and forgot everything that hadn't yet happened, until there wasn't any light left to see by and they knew each other only by feel.

Magniloquence

FAUSTUS MACELOVICH from the English Department had to come to the lecture by the Nobel Laureate, just as everyone did. He needed to appear in the crowd and shake hands with the other professors. This was far beyond his normal cheese Danish and crumblingly old book at the dining room table routine, where his recently dead wife looked down on him from a giant painting, done by Faustus himself upon their return from her first bad-news doctor appointment. This was a special night, a night on which each professor hoped to shake the hand belonging to the body belonging to such an important mind. They all knew that as they fell asleep that night, they would dream of their acceptance speech for that same storied award, remembering to thank the secretaries and the deans and the chairs and the chancellors and vice chancellors and the provost and the vice provost and the president, and vowing to always show up to each and every lecture they were to give, early, not like this ungrateful person. These professors knew that if they were honored they would never, never forget where they came from. They would arrive everywhere bearing gifts for their hosts. Beautiful fruit baskets, chocolates imported from villages so small they didn't even have names. What grateful, humble, well-deserved recipients they would be!

They now stood in the red-velvet-seated auditorium with many others from across the departments. The professors had all attended lectures here countless times: physicists, poets, ethnomusicologists, archivists. As usual, there were cookies and cheese and coffee urns and small paper cups. As usual, they cordialed and greeted and congratulated and acted nice whether or not it was sincere. Faustus endured the sympathy for his lost wife from some and appreciated it from others and was avoided by many who did not know what to say.

He had practiced for this, his reintroduction. He had read the sports page and was armed with knowledge of the baseball season and the basketball draft. He had prepared a list of conversation topics. "This new pitcher the Dodgers have, what a terrible choice," he would say, "but I do think the center from Duke has incredible potential," and even, "Won't you join me in moving to Canada if the Republicans win next year?" He feared asking others about their spouses and children, because he did not want to have to speak about his own family.

It did not used to be hard, this place where his life-life and his work-life met up. Aside from committees and meetings and budgets taking up ever more time, he had always felt like one of the rare men to be completely fulfilled. He used to arrive on time to all the faculty parties and watch his wife across the room make intelligent, witty remarks to the delight of senior members of his department. Sometimes he thought Petra was as responsible for his making tenure as he himself was. Now that she was gone, he did not know how to stand in this room right. He looked around at the familiar faces, some people he had known for decades, and was filled with the sense of being incomplete—not enough of a person to do his job. He was paid for his mind, but at this moment he did not know how to find his mind within the shimmering sorrow of his heart. The questions he had spent his career considering seemed like kickable little stones compared to the topography of this loss.

He had counted on the cookies to be enough to get him through the milling period, but this was getting to be an unusually long one. In the lecture hall, the professors began to tire of milling. They wanted to sit down. They wanted at this hour to listen and, many of them, to doze. This was supposed to be the reward—a place where everyone believed as they did—after days spent laboring in classrooms, waving their arms, each wave a misunderstood expression of their love of the subject: a mathematical wave, a wave to the beauty of the Principles of Physics. The slippery-eyed students in their straight rows, the visible boredom surrounding them in gray clouds, asked, "But, Professor," adjusting their miniskirts or basketball shorts, "how many academic sources do we need?"

"We should really be getting started," the professors began to say to one another. "Isn't someone in charge here?" Except for a few wiry-haired ex-hippies, the professors tended to be watch-watching on-timers. Lateness was a sign of laziness and unwillingness to attend to The Way Things Must Go.

Faustus took his cookies to a corner seat, alone and with a bad view. "I am at school," he whispered to himself. "This is fine." He thought about the last day he taught a class and the doctor's appointment following it. After, Petra and Faustus had parked their newish car on the street and walked into the house, whereupon Petra took a slow and silent lap, touching each item on each shelf. The Native American pots from trips to the Southwest. The pictures of their nieces and nephews. A hammer left on the mantel after hanging a picture. The sun was still strong and it broke into the house in tubes of light so that his wife, her fingers moving slowly over item after item, was bright white.

A woman sat down next to Faustus and introduced herself as Professor Claire Baker, Bio. They had little in common once they established that he was childless and hadn't even passed his high school science classes. And in regard to reading, Professor Baker admitted to enjoying a *People* magazine on the beach but preferred no words to words. "Written words, that is. Talking I like, I can talk plenty of words!" She was visibly amused by her bad sentence, as if it was a shining testament to her identity as a Science Person. "See that?" she joked. Faustus saw that. "You? What's your story?" she asked.

"My wife is dead and I'm taking the semester off," he said, too tired to recall the manners he had promised himself to employ. "But I think the center from Duke has amazing potential."

"Oh, you poor thing," she began, but he interrupted her.

"What I would like to do?" he said. "Is for us both to pretend that I am invisible."

At this point, an ambitious undergraduate—feeling the anxiety of this late start, the anxiety of the absence of the great speaker all the way from Oxford whom he knew all the professors had been waiting to meet, professors in whose minds he

could picture perfect questions formulated over the last weeks—
went to the podium and tapped the microphone. "Hello, everybody," he said. He clapped his hands together dramatically and
projected his voice much more than necessary, so that every
time he said the letter *P*, a great explosion of sound went out
through the seats.

"Please, please, settle down. Welcome to this evening's pro-
gram. I think we ought to get started, don't you?" He swished
his hand through his thick brown hair. "Um . . . Learning is important, I think we can all agree. So, I think that this university is a great institution. Actually all universities, but this one
in particular." The undergraduate was already running out of
things to say and he hadn't said anything yet. He had hoped
that his presence at the podium would root out the Laureate,
who might stand up graciously and wait to be introduced. No
such graciousness occurred, so the undergraduate continued.
"Uh, when I arrived here I didn't care about the Spanish Civil
War. Maybe other people always cared, but I didn't. But now,
because of Professor Paul Pretoria's class this semester, I think
it's *awesome*. Oh!" he said, getting an idea, "please put your
hands together for Professor Paul Pretoria."

Professor Baker and Faustus both clapped, but they did not
look at each other.

In order to come to the stage, Professor Pretoria had to
squeeze past the knees of a half row of people. "What an unex-
pected honor," he said when he finally arrived. "Thank you,
Carlo. I haven't prepared anything, but as long as I have you
here I might like to say a few words about . . ." Whatever he actually said, what nearly all the other professors heard was "the

capture of so and so which I will relate to the events of blah blah and to the unusual situation we find ourselves in concerning blank."

The speech was certainly more than a few words. The many wrists were busy with watch viewings. "Have you seen the Nobel Laureate?" people asked. "Maybe he's late? Maybe he's stuck in traffic? Maybe he's lost or dead or asleep? But what could be more important than this?" they asked. "His peers have gathered out of respect and admiration, and there is no better honor than that. Certainly, no personal problem could ever matter more."

After points and counterpoints, evidence and notes on the evidence, Professor Pretoria, nervous and sweating with the excitement of his own argument, suddenly looked up and realized that no one was listening. The entire university faculty, gathered here, was bored by what he had imagined might be his own Nobel Prize–winning theory. He said quietly and with a heave of despair directed at a sleeping man in the second row, "This brings me to the next speaker this evening: the amazing, exceptional, *genius* Professor Zelk." His voice was burned sugar.

Bill Zelk woke up to the sound of his own name ringing through the speakers. No notes of sarcasm sounded to him. What a wonderful way to wake up! He squirmed and adjusted his wire-rimmed glasses eight times on the way to the stage, making some who did not know him think he perhaps had some sort of disorder. The psychologists were certain. "I am involved in the study of mole rats," he said. "We are looking at the act of fecal perfuming." He looked out at the crowd. "There is an awful lot to say on the subject," and he began to say it.

. . .

FOR THE FIRST FULL HOUR, the professors, Faustus among them, sat up straight in the auditorium chairs, some with legs crossed at the knee, some at the ankle. They had listened vaguely to each introduction and clapped as the next bespectacled or mustachioed person took the stage. Occasionally some got up and had a bit of refreshment. The respectful professors remained quiet even while chewing their cheese.

By hour two they began to fidget. They continued to scan the room for unfamiliar faces—prize-winning faces, the face of the smartest breed. They pointed through the spaces between heads, hopeful that they had found the guest. Faustus had no intention of trying to pick the Laureate out, worried he might ask someone he should have recognized. Perhaps someone with whom he had had a nice conversation at last year's Christmas Party about Yeats's dog.

No one wanted to be the first to give up. They hoped that after such turmoil must come great treasure. Whatever sense it made or didn't, the longer they stayed the more they felt they must continue to do so. They did take other liberties. Most of the French Department curled up on the floor under their seats and napped. They looked like a series of tortoises, their black sweaters hiding the pink of their skin. Others went back to earlier discussions with one another, always with one eye on the podium in case one of two things happened: they themselves were called up to speak, or the headliner finally arrived.

Words like "venerable" and "inimitable" and "indefatigable" were said so many times they began to sound made up. After an analysis of subjectivity and objectivity in Poe and Dickinson, Professor Sydney Mott looked out at the mess of a room and said, "I've been divorced recently, as some of you know. She took the cat and I took the fish." He wondered out loud whether his teen-age daughter was sleeping with her boyfriend and whether he ought to try to stop her if she was. "He isn't even that cute, the boyfriend," he explained. "He has a mustache. And my daughter is such a beauty, Botticelli-esque." The professors itched at this microphoned admission. Things like this occurred in creative writing departments, maybe in art, certainly drama, but this was none of those. They did not know what to do.

In the back, the coffee ran out. The cookies were eaten, although a few were secreted away in the corduroy pockets of professors who thought ahead to future hunger. They fingered them in there, little disks of survival. In the back of the room was a cluster of historians and poets talking about what a nice round number one hundred was. Faustus stood behind them and listened.

"You know," said the same undergraduate who had started things off, "Wilt Chamberlain claimed to have had a hundred illegitimate children." In this moment that was beautiful to the historians and to the poets.

"They should get them all together for a game sometime. They could sing the national anthem," someone offered.

"They could file into the basketball court in a long line—just think how tall they would be—all of them wearing their father's jersey."

"And the announcer's voice would echo through the build-ing: 'Ladies and gentlemen, boys and girls, please rise for the singing of the national anthem by The Illegitimate Children of Wilt Chaimberlain.'"

"They could sing it in a round," someone else added.

"And all their mothers, who number almost as many, could come out and harmonize."

"That would be an historical event," the historians agreed.

"That would be a poetic event," the poets added.

Some of the members of the French Department touched each other's black tights, both parties pretending not to be awake.

Claire Baker approached Faustus and took him by the arm. "If you would please come over here, please, I promise we won't try to talk to you." She sat him down in a circle of German Romanticists. An older woman, long established in the department, put the bottle of water she was holding down in the center of the circle. "Spin," she said to Faustus. "As long as we're here."

"Is this what I think it is?" Faustus asked.

"We're all waiting for something great to happen in here," the woman answered. Faustus spun and the mouth of the bottle pointed directly back at him.

"Spin again," Professor Baker said. On his second spin, the bottle pointed to a woman whose hair, skin and dress were nearly the same shade of brownish pink.

"I think you are trying to do me a favor," he said to the circle. The woman looked up at him through her square bangs and smiled, rocking forward onto her hands and knees. He turned his face and offered his cheek to her. She put her lips to his skin and held them there. They were warm and full of questions.

. . .

PEOPLE HAD COME to the funeral heavy with flowers. Faustus stood in the circle with the others—people from the department, people from the neighborhood, cousins. His and Petra's parents were all dead or too senile to travel, and the two of them had no children. Faustus wished in that moment for someone who felt the loss more than he. He wished for a daughter, eyelids swollen from crying, whom he could put his arm around and comfort, whom he could drive home, where they would sit in the dark of the living room and listen carefully to the absence of their wife and mother. Just hear the house without her.

Faustus had read a poem by Ezra Pound over the hole in the ground and each of the gathered people stooped down and took a handful of dirt to throw on the lowered box. The earth accepted Petra in and the living made their way inside, where they stood together reducing the hill of a vegetable platter and talking in voices much quieter than necessary. The guests stayed long enough to prove that they were willing to give up their Sunday afternoon even though it was a beautiful day, even though it was getting close to summer. If any of them had plans for tennis later or for barbecues, they did not let it show. Faustus imagined them that evening in their various backyards refusing plates of grilled chicken, saying, "I wish I hadn't eaten so much at that *funeral*."

Like the rest of the guests, Faustus finally went home. He let himself into the house and sat down with his back against the door, where the tiles were cool on his legs and he tried to hear, as he had earlier imagined, every single thing that his wife was not doing in their home on this Sunday night. He could hardly keep track of it all, she was so busy being absent. She was not pouring water into a glass or a pitcher. She was not kicking his shoes out of the hall. She was not switching the laundry into the dryer. She was not opening the screen door and going outside barefoot and calling for him to come look at the sunset. She was not putting lotion on her elbows or flattening the newspaper or picking up the ringing telephone, which would go on calling out the absence of Petra in nine-ring sequences dozens of times every day.

EVENTUALLY, most of the cookie-savers ate their cookies. They sneaked off into dark corners or pretended to sneeze, quickly stuffing the crunchy morsel into their mouths. They did not want to be spotted and have to share. One woman, an administrator in the Composition Department who wanted her saved cookie to last a long time, held it flat against her palm and licked it over and over like a popsicle.

An African filmologist approached the podium. He wore denim shorts and white socks pulled all the way up to his knees and a sport coat. He had three watches on, all of which told him that it was late and he was tired. He said just a few words, then began that practiced acceptance speech for whichever prize he might someday be awarded. "I want to thank you for this in-credible honor. When I was a boy, I sneaked into the cinema one afternoon and, in a way, I have never left that dark room full of magic." The professors let his speech drift in and around them.

To hear him thank his mother the way he did, and the teachers of his youth, felt as though they were all thanking their mothers and the teachers of their youth. He leaned his forehead on the wooden surface of the podium and fell asleep like that, his arms up around his head, the dream of acknowledgment hovering above. The microphone was on, and the in and out of his breathing was amplified through the whole room.

"Tell me if something happens," the professors said to one another, and everyone closed their eyes. Some lay on the shoulders of others, drooling onto the tweed or houndstooth. Some slept in piles on the floor like puppies. Some found places alone. A Religious Studies lecturer sucked her thumb. Someone turned off the lights, and since there were no windows, the auditorium was completely dark.

Faustus and the rest of the spin-the-bottlers lay down in a circle like toppled dominoes, each head finding rest on a foreign set of legs. Faustus's right ear was suctioned to the monochromatic woman's bare calf. The calf did not make noises the way a stomach might. It must have been busy in there, distributing blood to each sinew of muscle, but it did so in silence.

He could not see it, but in the dark around him, some players held hands, sweaty and excited. Faustus looked into the dark and tried to make a list of reasons for existing. Kissing was on there, and so were hollandaise sauce and racquetball.

Suddenly he felt a hand on his face, its digits and palm covering most of his features. It was not a gentle touch, exactly. He felt he was the ocean floor and this was an exploratory machine out to map his exact topography. He tried to breathe consistently in order not to throw off the findings. The curious hand stuck three of its fingers into his mouth, and he sucked them like a baby. Faustus was desperately close to believing that the fingertips belonged to Petra, that if he followed them to the hand, wrist and arm, he would find his wife's body there. All her inner workings clean and polished. He did not move the hand for a long time. He let it sit, heavy on his chin, while all around him, around all of them, the amplified breathing rattled out from the speakers.

But the fingers were unknown and, he checked, ringless. He carefully moved the hand away, placing it on top of its outstretched twin. He extracted himself from the circle and went to the podium, where he held the African filmologist in his own arms and began to talk quietly into the microphone.

"I have been weeding around the Johnny-jump-ups and watering the apricot tree. Yesterday the poppies were looking droopy, so I gave them extra water and they perked right up. It was amazing how quickly they reacted. Remember how the upstairs toilet was starting to leak? I think it's finally time to replace it. I went to the store last weekend, but I couldn't decide what to buy. I needed your help. All toilets are ugly and all toilets have the same gross function and I don't know how to prefer one over another. You would have had a much less emotional reaction to this problem. I also wish you had been there to harvest the basil. And I've been reading Chekhov, whom I know you love. Food and books and shit, I guess that's what you're missing."

If anyone was awake, they did not make a sound. Faustus said, "I'm not making a very good argument for your return. I promise that if you were here, I would not make you go to the hardware store. If you were here, I would set you up in the yard with a blanket and a glass of iced tea to watch the hummingbirds hover over the sweet syrup in the feeder. You would never have to move if you didn't want to." He looked at his left hand, the ring around and around his finger.

"Petra, people tell me I will 'move on' and I can't believe it. But if it does ever happen, and I forget to feel this pressing absence of you, if I make it through a meaningless party and don't remember to hate everyone for their peaceful lives until the morning, please know that I am already sorry. I am going to try to be brave like you asked me to, but I don't have any idea yet what that means. Is it braver to allow the sadness of your leaving to spread into each of my bones until it is as big as you were to me? Or is it braver to let you drift out into what may very well be a brighter, finer place than this and be happy to think of your joy there? I hope, Petra, that I get it right."

He hung the filmologist back over the podium like a drying suit. Faustus did not return to the monochromatic woman and her exploring hand. And he did not leave or try to leave. He was glad to be able to fall asleep shrouded by the breath of so many others, and he did so curled up under the dessert table.

HOURS LATER, with arms draped over other arms and heads nested in the smalls of unfamiliar backs, the professors began to awaken. They made small noises and licked their dry lips. There was no light to see where they were, or who they were lying on. They were hungry. They began to freak out.

"Darkness!" someone yelled.

"Who am I?" one philosopher shouted. The professors climbed over one another like blind worms. They clawed at their own faces in dramatic fashion. For some, this was very satisfying. They felt that they might have a story to tell, a story of insanity and confusion, of terror and, they hoped, of survival. There was a certain disappointment when the buzzing of the fluorescent lights came on and all their wrinkles and mussed hair was revealed in one startling moment.

They looked around and realized with some sadness that they were not refugees or prisoners of war locked in a shabby cell someplace in Africa after having been arrested for their daring, dangerous thoughts. They were not forgotten miners trapped in the coal-black darkness of a tunnel in Kentucky. They were not persecuted intellectuals in a country that valued only hockey and civil war. The professors recognized the school logo on the coffee urns and on the podium. They recognized the nicely reupholstered seats. They recognized one another. Those who had kissed regretted it. Those who had spooned on the floor regretted it less, but still felt some embarrassment, particularly if they had been the Baby Spoon, and the Mama Spoon had been from their own department.

Suddenly, the undergraduate opened the big double door to the outside. The world had been right there, four small inches of squeaky metal away. The professors spilled out into the light. They imagined violin music getting louder as they exited, their arms raised over their heads, praising salvation and daylight. Around them, students were on their way to class. Some even recognized teachers they had had. Teachers whose hair was sticking up all over. Some of whom had their shirts one button off.

Faustus came back awake to the sound of the freed men and women. He was lying on his shirt, his uneaten cookie crushed in his breast pocket. A huge river of light washed into the room, whiting everything out for Faustus, whose eyes had gotten used to dimness.

Tributaries

THE GIRLS ARE WORMED OUT across the floor under down comforters even though daytime is hardly over, trying to get a jump-start on the slumber party. "My parents both have perfect love-arms," Genevieve tells her friends. "Both of them can write. They write love letters to each other. It's almost sick." No one thinks this is sick. Everyone wants this. Pheenie, Marybeth, Sara P. and Sara T. all want to have the proof.

Though the girls know many two-armers, even some who seem happy and in love, what they talk about are those with love-grown arms. "My mom doesn't have anything and my dad just has fingers growing out of his chest. He can't control them and they grab at anything that is close enough," says Pheenie.

"My grandmother has seven, but she was always married to my grandfather. She says she fell in love with him over and over," Sarah T. adds. Seven is an unusual number. Two sometimes, maybe three, but past that something important must have gone wrong. And still, the girls are greeted every morning by the television news anchors, their teeth white, their hair unyielding and their single, perfect love-grown arms, offering no hint of uncertainty.

Sarah P. lowers her head. "My dad's arm keeps growing. It drags on the floor. It is soft and he can wrap it up and tie it in a knot."

Genevieve, putting her hand on Sarah P.'s sleeping-bag-burrowed body, says, "I wonder what mine will be like. I want to have two. I think it's better to fall in love twice, once to try it out and twice to know for sure. I want the first arm to be a stump and the second to be full grown."

"I only want one. I only want one perfect one." Pheenie shakes her head.

The girls go quiet and all the arms of all the loves they do not have yet beat silent beneath their skin. They thump and prepare.

AFTER ALL THE STUDENTS save the detentioners have left the building for the weekend, Principal Kevin again tells the story of his love. His wife's beauty surpasses the Louvre, the Sistine. Both his secretaries chirp. They wide-eye his love-grown arm and tilt their heads and wish for what he has.

"You might not know what it feels like, but I do," he tells them, "and it's *terrific*."

In fact, Principal Kevin stuffs his third sleeve. He stuffs it, but no one at school knows he does. The sleeve is filled with a prosthetic, a real fake arm commissioned from the lab at the hospital. It screws onto a threaded metal disc implanted on his chest. At the write end: a stump. The stump is sewn up to look like the hand has been amputated. Principal Kevin is smart enough to know that a fake hand looks fake, and instead of giving up the whole beautiful vision, he tells a story about a kitchen fire in which he saved his wife and daughter but his third hand, his lovely third hand, was burned to a crisp.

But Principal Kevin knows himself. He is sure that if he *did* have a love arm, and if he *had* lost the hand to it, he would have wanted a replacement. It's the kind of man he is—everything in its place. So, attached to the very real-looking stump with big, obvious screws, is a wooden hand. It is the fakest he could find, an art class model. Against this, the arm looks especially lifelike.

When he comes to the end of the story, one he has told more than once to everyone he has ever met, he manually straightens the jointed wooden fingers and brushes them against each of his secretary's right cheeks. "The hand burned," he muses, "but the arm resisted. The arm did not even singe."

FEW OF PRINCIPAL KEVIN'S STUDENTS, his daughter Genevieve among them, have any love-arm development. The girls check constantly in the bathroom between classes, inviting each other to inspect the soft skin of their side-body for bumps. They say they are falling in love, not with the specifics of one boy, but with the idea that such a thing is possible—that they belong to a species built to snap together in everlasting pairs. They feel themselves falling in love with the entirety of the opposite gender, with their own blooming selves, but their bodies do nothing to corroborate. Their skeletons are stubborn and unchanged.

For the boys, any new protrusions would be bad for their social standing. Unless they are extremely religious and plan on a just-legal wedding, an unmoved form is an asset. Certain other anatomical parts have made some very favorable changes, but love can't break the seal. After high school this changes. Older brothers are proud of their arms. They sit on thrift store couches, where girlfriends rub lotion onto the new branches and kiss them and want to make love so often because there is proof that what they have is real, that something has changed because of it. They lie close in a twin bed afterward and put their extra arms side by side. They let the unfinished appendages warm each other up just by pressing.

DURING AFTER-SCHOOL DETENTION, Miss C lectures about Amelia Earhart because she wants to and the audience can't go anywhere. She zooms herself around the room like an airplane making swooping turns between desks. She is a two-armer, but that's not the whole story. From the waist up, she is covered in hands. Dozens. Under the cover of clothing, their fingers move and stretch and wriggle. Sixteen sixteen-year-olds keep out of her way until she drops suddenly and kneels under a desk. "Blammo," she says in a loud whisper. "I'm gone, disappeared, just like that." She does not move for a long moment. Chairs squeak. Students hiss. Miss C remains disappeared at a pair of sneakered feet. The boy reaches down like it is an accident and touches her head. He can feel her skybound heat.

When she stands up, she is rippling, the fingers twitter beneath her blouse. After the bell, in the hall, the boy sticks his chest out and imitates with his two original hands. "Oh, Amelia Earhart, I want to jump your bones," he squawks.

Miss C sticks her head out the door. "You've got a poker face now," she tells him, "but your body will give you away soon enough."

THE HIGH SCHOOL BOYS keep rubber gloves in their wallets and inflate them when they want to try to win a girl over. They tuck them under their shirts and let the bulging, breath-warm air-fingers reach out at their dates, indicating what could be.

Of course, the girls know the hands are stand-ins. But when the boys say, *I could really develop feelings*, and they have the visual aid, and when the music pumping out of the speakers has someone singing a harmony and someone singing a melody, the drapery of their clothing is easily removed, and their desperately hopeful limbs cross and twist and hold.

EVEN PRINCIPAL KEVIN'S HOME MAIL comes addressed to Principal Kevin. On this Friday, while he waits for his wife to come home and remove his arm so that he can enjoy the evening unencumbered, he spreads the envelopes out on the table until the whole surface is covered with his name. They ask, *Please, if you could spare some money for the children.* Say, *Do you have any idea what kind of excellent interest rate you deserve?* They report the therms used to keep the house warm, the wife's desires made known to him by her spending on the platinum credit card. A note from his daughter: *Dad, I love you and I'm at*

Pheenie's for the night.—Genevieve. He is alone with the facts of his existence and it makes him tired. Just looking at the debts and balances.

His wife comes in from her exercise class and she finds him here, wilted. He looks at her and picks the prosthetic up with his good left hand like a bone. *Look what I found, take this from me, I have been waiting.*

"You could have done it yourself," she says.

"It's yours. I want you to do it."

"We have the PTA meeting tonight," she reminds him, kissing the arm as if it were real. As if it does not whisper to her that her eyes to him are tiny emptiness and her hair a strangle of ropes and her heart a flicked, rolling marble.

"Will you go in my place? Tell them it's a headache. I just want a nap and a break." She kneels on the floor in front of him and takes his shirt off, then twists the arm to the left. The elbow bends as she unscrews, so the arm faces in all the wrong directions.

She puts the arm down on a chair, brushing the hair so it faces in one direction like windblown wheat. She kisses his cheek and returns him to his kingdom of bills. She comes back a moment later with a cloth to wipe clean the metal threads of the attachment, both innie and outtie. They get sweat-damp throughout the day. A shimmer of salt crusts the edges. She dries. She oils and dries again.

She does not take care of his fake love-arm with her real one. She lets that sit against her side, the fingers spread out against her, quiet and still. It is her born-on hands she tends to him with, just as he tends to her with his.

. . .

PRINCIPAL KEVIN'S ARM needs caring for like leather does. Cleaning and mink oil. While he sits with his mail, his wife takes it with her into the bathtub and lets it float there while she washes herself, her triangles and spheres and nubs, and her own third arm, this one very real. She cleans both authentic and created with extra-gentle baby shampoo. The wooden hand is heavily waxed, and water beads, then scrambles off, as if afraid. She closes her eyes and leans back against her twisted-up hair, the prosthetic floating limp on the surface of the water, a ship stuck in a tiny, unleavable sea.

"Good bath?" he asks, naked, from the bed when she comes out. The sun shoots off the metal hole in his chest and blinds her. She tightens her robe and turns away, places his arm on a stand by his dresser, where it stretches straight, pointing out the window at the bug-buzzing evening.

"You know you are my peach," he says to her. "Come and sit." He strokes what she has grown for him. It is elbow length but unjointed and has a hand, always carefully manicured. He pushes the cuticles back. "My love is bigger than any limb," he tells her.

"What is mine then?"

THE BOYS LIKE TO WATCH Miss C walk down the hall, all those hands and fingers moving together under her clothes, beckoning. This evening, when she makes a trip back and forth to her car, the football team turns from the field where the lowering winter sun skates the grass pink. They watch her search in her bag for keys, which come out glinting. Her hair picks up the light the usual way, but it is her body that receives it in waves, like she is the surface of the ocean and all the water inside is angling for a peek at the great open space of the sky.

Miss C is really named Claribel. She goes into her office alone with the blinds down, door locked, grading papers shirtless before the PTA gets started. Her hands hold things for her: red, blue, green pens. Paper clips and sticky notes. Her breasts are surrounded by a ring of four hands each and look like lakes in a forest, calm, quiet, protected. While she scratches at the paper, the hands clean each other's nails. They hook fingers.

PRINCIPAL KEVIN'S WIFE also has her own name, which is Jan. She is a committed mother and she has excellent legs. Both are goals she has been able to meet. While the prom committee presents its plan for an Antarctic theme, Claribel leans over and whispers to Jan, "You've got great legs." She is a fan of this appendage, a limb that does not sprout up but comes exclusively with the original configuration, and always in one matched pair. "Your daughter is a real contributor lately," she adds.

Jan humbles her head but knows it is true. "I am proud of her. I think it's hard to be the principal's daughter."

"He's such an admirable man."

"Sure."

When the meeting is over, they go up to Claribel's office for a coffee, look out the small window at the football field. The team practices in the dark for a game they need to win. The women talk about teaching and administration. They talk about the graduating class and where they will go to college. Jan's extra hand emerges out a lavender cuff with a pearl button.

"Your nails look nice," Claribel remarks. "I have too many hands to take that on. It would cost me thousands of dollars."

"That would be quite a project," Jan admits. A flock of black-birds rushes by and they call out to one another. Jan can see her car in the parking lot waiting to take her home, where she will find her husband on the couch, devouring popcorn and laughing loudly at the commercials, and this thought makes her stomach sink. "You know what? I'll do them for you," Jan says. "Your nails. Let's do them."

Claribel resists the way people do. "No, no. There are too many," but already she is unbuttoning her shirt from the bottom up.

WHEN IT IS FINALLY DARK, the girls take their clothes off and go in the pool, splash in the hot blue of that gathered liquid. Their skins are a wet slick. Their hair goes pointy and water falls from it in straight beaded lines. "I want to love you guys forever," they say to the half-lit faces. The new breasts reach out to sniff at the world they will inhabit.

The girls get into the bathtub together, all five, because it is a big one and they are cold. They wash one another's backs with soap that smells like lilacs. Legs slip against legs. The names of the boys they want to love fall out of their mouths.

Dry but not yet dressed, Genevieve takes out a permanent marker. She draws parallel lines down the center of her chest and then the five loopy fingers of a hand at the end. She writes *Cole P.* inside the wrist. Pheenie turns away and says, "Draw one on my back." Pretty soon they are covered in the outlines of limbs ending in digits. Some drawings are realistic, the arcs of knuckles and nails. Some are more like paws, round and imprecise. The girls sleep in a pile, the scent of the marker sharp on their skin.

In the morning, the original drawings will be printed again on whatever skin was pressed there; even their cheeks will be ghosted with imaginings of love.

As the shirt comes open, the fingers beneath stretch themselves out, crack their knuckles. Claribel lies down on her back hands.

"Who is this hand for?" Jan asks, filing the first nails.

"That's Abe Lincoln and next to that is my father. Those were the first two. They grew when I was eighteen and I went to Washington for the summer. I sat on the steps of the Lincoln Memorial and read his biographies. I watched the lump grow to a ball, and then a wrist. The fingers started the same way, lumps and then balls." Jan massages a jewel of lotion in the palm. "My father called to tell me he was leaving to live in Kentucky with a new woman. *I love you even though I don't love your mother,* he told me, and right then, all at once, this hand erupted out of my chest."

They go on. Eleanor Roosevelt, Tom Sawyer. Ms. Earhart. A younger cousin who died in a flood. Men whom she knew for weeks sometimes, hours sometimes, before an appendage began where they touched her and they took their coats and left. "Some of them did not know I loved them. Many of them were dead. I have never known which ones were real, or if all of them were. I have hands that showed up without my ever knowing who they were hoping to touch or hold."

Jan thinks about this, about her body's agreement to tell the same story she does: love right away, love still, love always. "I think it's wonderful that you have loved so much," she says. "You've given your whole body over to it. We award medals for much less useful acts."

Claribel nods her head and feels the twitter of something beating beneath her skin wanting to exist. "But I have proof all over me that no one is alone in my heart. Everyone wants to be alone in someone else's heart. In the end, I am alone in mine."

As Jan works, Claribel's fingernails become red squares like windows into the coursing, blooded tributaries beneath, as if Jan has painted her way inside.

GENEVIEVE KNOWS that her father's arm is a fake. He likes to take it off when he gets home. He likes to eat his dinner without it in his way, to hug his daughter unimpeded. She does not admit this to her friends, because they believe that what her parents have is the lucky thing everyone hopes for. But it is the lie that Genevieve loves. That he built himself what did not come on its own. He said yes, and though his physical form stayed silent, he created a voice for it. Made it sing the notes of his song.

"MY HUSBAND'S ARM IS PLASTIC," Jan says, and the painted nails wink at her.

"Oh my god. But he talks about it all the time."

"I know."

"He must love you though."

"He must. But he also must not."

"Climb on," Claribel tells her. The many fingers reel her in.

"How I used to hold the kids on my feet?" Jan asks. She climbs on, laughing and nervous. Claribel lies on the mattress of her back hands, and Jan rests like a platter on the front. Their bodies are held apart. Air travels through the tunnels. Fingers dig themselves in. Jan puts her three arms out like wings to steady herself.

Outside, boys crash into each other and land in heaps.

"Here I am, held up by everyone you've loved," Jan says. "See that?"

When Jan begins to tip, Claribel tells her, "It's only because you are looking that you can't balance. Close your eyes. Close your eyes, because we've got you."

ALONE THIS EVENING, Principal Kevin takes his arm into bed. He lays it down and rubs up against it. He is naked. The hand stays open in a lazy wooden cup. It will only hold what is given. He takes it into his own, places it over himself, moves it around.

"I love you," he says out loud. "Do you know that? I love you."

If you say so, he feels the hand tell him. It is cool on his most delicate skin.

"We all do," he tells it. The hand is boss-able. If he wants to grind into it, it is grinded. "We all do," he repeats. "We all love."

Acknowledgments

Thank you to my teachers: Ron Carlson, Michelle Latiolais, Geoffrey Wolff, Christine Schutt, Brad Watson, Amy Gerstler, Doug Anderson, and Jackie Levering-Sullivan. My admiration is truly endless.

Thanks to my cohorts in Irvine who offered insight when these stories were still blind, bald little babies. Everything I've written since is better for having shared a table with you all.

Huge thanks to the magazine editors who gave some of these stories their first homes: Hannah Tinti and Maribeth Batcha, Cressida Leyshon and Deborah Treisman, Leslie Daniels, Carter Edwards, and Ben Mirov.

For PJ Mark—books and authors don't get better friends than you.

Every single person at Riverhead. Special thanks to Geoff Kloske, Sarah Stein, Kate Stark, Glory Plata, and Lydia Hirt. And to Sarah McGrath and Jynne Martin, magicians both.

My family. My friends. How unbelievably good you all are.

For generous support, tremendous thanks to Glenn Schaeffer, the International Center for Writing and Translation at UC Irvine, the Squaw Valley Community of Writers, the Tin House Writers' Conference, and the Bread Loaf Writers' Conference.

And to Teo—I love you from the Sangre de Cristo Mountains to the Mekong River, Balboa Island to the Gobi desert. From me and you to me and you and Clay. Let's always run away together.